W9-AOE-772

*Literary Lives*

General Editor: **Richard Dutton**, Professor of English, Lancaster University

This series offers stimulating accounts of the literary careers of the most admired and influential English-language authors. Volumes follow the outline of the writers' working lives, not in the spirit of traditional biography, but aiming to trace the professional, publishing and social contexts which shaped their writing.

*Published titles include:*

*Cedric C. Brown*
JOHN MILTON

*Peter Davison*
GEORGE ORWELL

*Richard Dutton*
WILLIAM SHAKESPEARE

*Jan Fergus*
JANE AUSTEN

*Caroline Franklin*
BYRON

*James Gibson*
THOMAS HARDY

*Kenneth Graham*
HENRY JAMES

*Paul Hammond*
JOHN DRYDEN

*Lisa Hopkins*
CHRISTOPHER MARLOWE

*W. David Kaye*
BEN JONSON

*Mary Lago*
E. M. FORSTER

*Clinton Machann*
MATTHEW ARNOLD

*Alasdair D. F. Macrae*
W. B. YEATS

*Joseph McMinn*
JONATHAN SWIFT

*Kerry McSweeney*
GEORGE ELIOT

*John Mepham*
VIRGINIA WOOLF

*Michael O'Neill*
PERCY BYSSHE SHELLEY

*Leonée Ormond*
ALFRED TENNYSON

*Harold Pagliaro*
HENRY FIELDING

*George Parfitt*
JOHN DONNE

*Gerald Roberts*
GERARD MANLEY HOPKINS

*Felicity Rosslyn*
ALEXANDER POPE

*Tony Sharpe*
T. S. ELIOT
WALLACE STEVENS

*Peter Shillingsburg*
WILLIAM MAKEPEACE THACKERAY

*Angela Smith*
KATHERINE MANSFIELD

*Grahame Smith*
CHARLES DICKENS

*Janice Farrar Thaddeus*
FRANCES BURNEY

*Linda Wagner-Martin*
SYLVIA PLATH

*Nancy A. Walker*
KATE CHOPIN

*Gary Waller*
EDMUND SPENSER

*Cedric Watts*
JOSEPH CONRAD

*John Williams*
MARY SHELLEY
WILLIAM WORDSWORTH

*Tom Winnifrith and Edward Chitham*
CHARLOTTE AND EMILY BRONTË

*John Worthen*
D. H. LAWRENCE

*David Wykes*
EVELYN WAUGH

**Literary Lives**
**Series Standing Order ISBN 0–333–71486–5 hardcover**
**Series Standing Order ISBN 0–333–80334–5 paperback**
(*outside North America only*)

You can receive future titles in this series as they are published by placing a standing order. Please contact your bookseller or, in case of difficulty, write to us at the address below with your name and address, the title of the series and one of the ISBNs quoted above.

Customer Services Department, Macmillan Distribution Ltd, Houndmills, Basingstoke, Hampshire RG21 6XS, England

# William Makepeace Thackeray

## A Literary Life

Peter Shillingsburg
*Professor of English*
*University of North Texas*
*USA*

First published 2001 by
PALGRAVE
Houndmills, Basingstoke, Hampshire RG21 6XS and
175 Fifth Avenue, New York, N. Y. 10010
Companies and representatives throughout the world

PALGRAVE is the new global academic imprint of St. Martin's Press LLC Scholarly and Reference Division and Palgrave Publishers Ltd (formerly Macmillan Press Ltd).

ISBN 0–333–65092–1 hardback
ISBN 0–333–65093–X paperback

This book is printed on paper suitable for recycling and made from fully managed and sustained forest sources.

A catalogue record for this book is available from the British Library.

Library of Congress Cataloging-in-Publication Data
Shillingsburg, Peter L.
William Makepeace Thackeray : a literary life / Peter Shillingsburg.
p. cm. — (Literary lives)
Includes bibliographical references and index.
ISBN 0–333–65092–1
1. Thackeray, William Makepeace, 1811–1863. 2. Novelists, English––19th century—Biography. I. Title: William Makepeace Thackeray. II. Title. III. Literary lives (New York, N.Y.)

PR5631 .S48 2000
823'.8—dc21
[B]

00–062602

10 9 8 7 6 5 4 3 2 1
10 09 08 07 06 05 04 03 02 01

Printed and bound in Great Britain by
Antony Rowe Ltd, Chippenham, Wiltshire

# Contents

# List of Figures

# Preface

William Makepeace Thackeray was born to British parents in Calcutta, India, on 18 July 1811. He died at age 52 in London on the night of 23 December 1863. He was both author and illustrator. The illustrations in this book are all by his hand, some taken from magazines, others from his own books and some from his letters. His most famous book in this century is *Vanity Fair*, first serialized in 1847–48. His most critically acclaimed work in the nineteenth century was *The History of Henry Esmond*, originally published in three volumes in 1852. His most popular work at the time was *The Newcomes*, serialized in 1853–55. Also considered major works are *The History of Pendennis*, serialized in 1848–50, *The Virginians*, serialized from 1857 to 1859, and *The Adventures of Philip*, serialized in 1861–62 in the *Cornhill Magazine*, of which Thackeray was the editor. Shorter novels that have received significant attention are *The Luck of Barry Lyndon*, serialized in 1844 in *Fraser's Magazine*, *Lovel the Widower*, serialized in 1860 in *The Cornhill*, and *Denis Duval*, left unfinished at his death and first published in 1864. His best known non-fiction includes travel books (*The Paris Sketch Book*, 1840; *The Irish Sketch Book*, 1843; *Notes of a Journey From Cornhill to Grand Cairo*, 1846; *The Book of Snobs*, 1846; and *The Roundabout Papers*, 1860–63), Christmas books – short stories, heavily illustrated and sometimes hand-coloured for the Christmas trade season (*Mrs. Perkin's Ball*, 1846; *Doctor Birch and His Young Friends*, 1849; *Rebecca and Rowena*, 1850; *The Kickleburys on the Rhine*, 1851; and *The Rose and the Ring*, 1855), and two important series of public lectures (*The English Humourists of the Eighteenth Century*, first delivered in 1852 and published in 1853, and *The Four Georges*, first delivered in 1855 and published in 1860).

This book is not a comprehensive or even chronological life of Thackeray. It is an introductory portrait of the author, a characterization of the 'speaker of the works', and an account of the relation between Thackeray's life and his works.

PLS

# Acknowledgements

I have incorporated several brief notes originally published in *The Thackeray Newsletter.*

I am grateful to my former students, Jeff Martin and Andrea Daniels, who read and commented on drafts of Chapters 6, 7 and 8. Thanks are due to Professors Judith Fisher, Edgar Harden and Miriam Shillingsburg for reading and helping to improve the whole manuscript. They should not be construed as endorsing the arguments or the emphases, but I am deeply grateful for their advice.

I dedicate this book to the person who helped me the most, not only by commenting on each part as it was written but also by being the representative of the audience to whom the book is addressed, and who by the by is an excellent daughter: Anne Carol Shillingsburg.

# 1
# Introduction

We often misconstrue what we hear because we do not know who is speaking. We do not know how to take what we read until we know who is writing. James Joyce's famous dictum about authors 'refining themselves out of existence' suggests that the text somehow should speak for itself, but in nineteenth-century fiction, particularly in that of William Makepeace Thackeray, the narrative voice more often than not is palpably present. One could say that of all the characters in *Vanity Fair* the narrator is (or perhaps narrators are) the most interesting in the book. This is a proposition totally lost on the makers of movie versions of the novel whose only technique with which to introduce the narrator is clumsy voice-overs. But the voices of the speaking narrators and the (silent) voice of the author that stands behind them make all the difference in a reader's perception of the story and the characters. Biography helps us to construct the persona and voice that speaks the fiction.

The facts of Thackeray's life have been chronicled thoroughly in Gordon Ray's meticulous and massive biography,[1] and the bulk of manuscript documents relevant to his life's story are published in six volumes of Thackeray's correspondence and private papers.[2] In the last 20 years six additional book-length biographical reconsiderations of Thackeray's life have appeared, laying out the chronology of his life and writings in conventional ways.[3] It seems unnecessary to do that again. But it does seem necessary and useful to attempt another portrait of Thackeray the writer. Our understanding of the writings is always influenced by our understanding of the writer – particularly, in Thackeray's case, our awareness of how his experiences in sex, money and religion shaped the man and the voices in which he wrote.

William Makepeace Thackeray remains interesting today because he had a literary life. We know a good deal about him, but we care about him because he wrote *Vanity Fair, Henry Esmond, The Book of Snobs, The Paris Sketch Book* and a few other remarkable stories and books. His domestic life, his religion, his financial failures and successes, his aspirations as an artist, his accomplishments as a book illustrator, his brief and failed political life, his investments in railroads and mining ventures, his victimization by failed Indian banks, his sexual escapades, his tragic marriage and his forlorn passion for his best friend's wife all have the interest and appeal inherent to any person's life. But above that ordinary appeal what matters about Thackeray is his literary life.

Although Thackeray's *Vanity Fair* was remade into television serials in each of the last three decades of the twentieth century, Thackeray has become the least-known star novelist from the Victorian era. He is also the least understood and least appreciated major writer of the time. Where once he was thought the rival of Charles Dickens both in art and in popular appeal, his writings now attract less than one-tenth the critical attention and perhaps less than one-hundredth of the popular attention devoted to the author of *Pickwick Papers* and *Great Expectations*. Anthony Trollope was early thought to be a thoroughly second-rate imitator of Thackeray and soon after his death fell almost entirely from public view, but Trollope is now more often read, more often viewed in TV and movie adaptations, and more often written about than his erstwhile master. The Brontës and George Eliot, who appealed to the same general readership as did Dickens and Thackeray, enjoy far more attention in classrooms and living rooms than WMT. Yet any student of Victorian fiction would readily acknowledge that Thackeray's *Vanity Fair* is one of the premier novels of the nineteenth century and that the author has equal claim to attention and standing with the writers who have now surpassed him in both general and academic appeal. No one hesitates to grant his superior claim to attention over Edward Bulwer, Charles Lever, Robert Surtees, Charles Read, Elizabeth Gaskell and George Meredith, to name a few of the most prominent 'second rung' novelists of those days.

There have been many attempts to explain Thackeray's 'fall from grace' in the public's – indeed, in the academy's – eyes. Some of these efforts place the blame on Thackeray, some on modern readers. Though I disagree with the assessment, against him it is said: He was wishy-washy in his morality, unimaginative in his plots, repetitious in his characters, unpleasant in his sneering satires, cloyingly sentimental in his nostalgias, maudlin in his cooings over babies and helpless women, vicious in his attacks on mothers-in-law, prejudiced and heartless in his portrayals of Blacks, Jews, the Irish and the French, and he was excessively sensitive and arrogant in person.[4] It has even been suggested, unworthily, that his selfish ego and social pride were evidenced in his banishing his wife to mental institutions and then placing her under the even cheaper care of a family whom he paid but did not visit.[5]

Critics less hostile and yet not charitable to Thackeray suggest that his works fail to appeal to modern readers because the dense allusiveness and thick texture of his prose – composed of current things, events and persons long since forgotten – have made it too difficult to understand the nuances and subtleties of his writing. The topicality of his vision, they say, mingled though it is with wise and clever universal portraits of humanity, makes his prose both appealing and repelling. Some modern readers attracted to Thackeray's humorous exposé of human foibles, find themselves sadly puzzled by off-hand references to long forgotten divas, tradesmen, politicians, dancers, saddlers, grocers, watchmakers, bankers, pawnbrokers, old-clothesmen, inns, coachmen and socially homogeneous (i.e. segregated) sections of London whose character has long since changed. Some of that may be true, but puzzlement arising from the modern reader's lack of knowledge may instead reflect misguided expectations about Thackeray and his writings.[6]

In recent times some critics more friendly to Thackeray have opposed these criticisms by affecting to admire the rigor and sharpness of Thackeray's early works, written in days when his personal losses made him sufficiently lean and hungry to be unmindful of what he might lose by impolitic observations or heterodox opinions. These critics admire the young Thackeray as a picaro, who stands outside the mainstream, like the child in the fairy tale proclaiming the emperor's new clothes non-existent, revealing conventional

*Figure 1.1* Self-portrait as narrator, *Vanity Fair*, 91

views to be sycophantic. According to this view, financial and social successes at mid-life spoiled the cub commentator and critic, drew his claws and incisors, and rendered the aging lion bland and non-threatening. Both the admiration and the disdain in this construction of Thackeray seem wayward, superficial and alien. They are the result of an unfortunate imposition of eccentric modern tastes on the body of Thackeray's distinctly Victorian yet distinctly individual achievements.[7]

Opinion about Thackeray's works has always been sharply divided between those who think of him as a dwindling Victorian light and those who still believe with Jane Welsh Carlyle, wife of the famous Victorian sage Thomas Carlyle, that 'Thackeray beats Dickens out of this world'. In the first group are many who claim to understand and agree with the justice of the author's declining reputation. They lament his failure 'to put his best foot forward', as Anthony Trollope put it.[8] They believe that Thackeray was his own worst enemy, that he vacillated in his morality, his artistic commitment, indeed, in his religious and political beliefs, and that he squandered the good will of readers by violating the sense of realism in fiction which his early works did so much to establish.

From the beginning, however, another group of readers has understood Thackeray differently. They see a writer whose keen observation of the foibles of society was tempered by an equally sharp awareness of his own complicity in its human weaknesses. They see a man who distrusted certainty and righteousness because of the mischief frequently done in the name of virtue. To them Thackeray appears to prefer to admit doubts and to tolerate the 'sins' of others rather than to set himself up as the judge who knows (i.e. pretends to know) what the world needs. They see a writer whose voice is sometimes detached and ironic and other times marked by humility and compassion. And they find in these contraries and contradictions an attractive complexity. In Thackeray's hands the tangle of ordinary life is not grounds for confusion and defeat but for acknowledging our own aspirations and weaknesses in the aspirations and weaknesses of others. He neither idolized heroes nor dismissed villains; for they are, like ourselves, a mixed lot. These critics see in Thackeray a writer whose wisdom transcends the oversimplifications and trivialities of popular fiction.

Thackeray was both a man of his time and out of it. He exposed the corruption and self-indulgence of luxury, but he was a person who loved luxury and self-indulgence. He led the writers of his age in realistic portrayals of character and society, but he deliberately undermined the illusion of reality by reminding his readers periodically that by reading they were participating in a fictive world. Among the novels by Victorians, Thackeray's most effectively blur the seam between fiction and history. His heroes are ordinary men, his villains are human, his good women are selfish, his hardhearted women are kind and intelligent, his husbands are tyrants who do not know any better, his wives are victims who court victimization without realizing it, his puppets are made of flesh and blood. Only his mothers-in-law are irredeemably mean-spirited. His narrative voices, particularly those of the voice-overs or so-called intruding commentaries, draw readers effectively into the fictive world of his characters; yet the author never lets readers forget the real world of story-telling and the marketing of fiction. In short, Thackeray's views of society, psychology and the economic dynamics of novel writing and publishing are so complex that readers in search of simple satisfactions and coherent order are often puzzled and disappointed.

Consequently one must learn to read Thackeray. His fiction is as topically allusive as that of any Victorian writer. As his age and culture recede in time, becoming more and more alien, young readers find it increasingly difficult to read his works at all, let alone richly, thickly and with enjoyment. Thackeray's knowledge of history was tremendous and his view of his own time was richly entwined with his view of history. The fictional worlds from his imagination coexist with the historical and contemporary worlds; the resulting emotional and intellectual soup is complex, subtle, thoughtful, and profoundly philosophical and moral. That many persons react badly or feebly to his works is not surprising, given the allusiveness of his prose and, more important, the sly cleverness of his narrative technique.

Furthermore, Thackeray's imitators have made his greatest accomplishments (realism and the ironic voice) passé for modern readers, who must learn what prose fiction was like for his contemporaries in order best to see the innovations of Thackeray's writing. The conventions of his time for both historians and novelists encouraged narratives that glossed the seamier side of life, offering either model behaviors to imitate or unfortunate episodes to avoid. History for historians, and individual lives for biographers and novelists, were progressions in which the lessons of the past helped to advance mankind by giving lessons to be learned and mistakes not to repeat. Life was a progress. One unfortunate result of such views is that they accidentally encouraged as normal and good what we now view, with the help of writers like Thackeray, as hypocrisy: moral fables predominated over detached or comic observations of ordinary life. At mid-century the Victorian public was not ready for the naturalism of an Edmund Gosse or the experimentation of a James Joyce, but a significant segment of society was ready to have common immoralities, domestic deceptions, and the injustices of conventional behavior acknowledged realistically and, indeed, irreverently. Modern writers have gone far in the directions first indicated by Thackeray, making some of his achievements seem tame.

Although his frequent references to things now forgotten may leave modern readers wondering if they have missed something, Thackeray was a consummate stylist, renowned from his day to this for the clarity and ease of his prose. The difficulty is not in his syntax or vocabulary, both of which are graceful and erudite. Nor is the problem primarily the unfamiliarity of the people, places and things in his fictional world. The main problem modern readers have in understanding and appreciating Thackeray's work is with the subtle complexity of voices, most successfully and dexterously played out in *Vanity Fair*, but inherent in the multiple pseudonymous works of his early years, and in the maddeningly deceptive voice of Arthur Pendennis, the narrator of the later works.

To know a person or a writer well is to know how to take what that person says. We allow our friends and close acquaintances a far wider range of voices than we allow strangers or persons with whom our relations are strained or hostile. The conventions of polite discourse and diplomatic exchange are narrow and highly controlled in order to diminish the chances of being misconstrued. Familiarity allows the relaxation of these narrow limits. A reader's reaction to a writer is controlled by the limits of sympathy and tolerance one is able to grant to the writer. Thackeray's writings address the reader in so many voices and with such confidence that conventional politeness between writer and reader is stretched.

That is not to say readers must surrender their critical faculties in order to understand Thackeray. The opposite is true. Naïve dependence on the reliability of the artist or narrator is sure to fail with Thackeray who speaks best to readers who have firm confidence in their own ability to sort through layers of irony and indirection, who delight in the ability of language to both hide and reveal the self-deceptions and attempted deceptions of others that every person practices with one degree or other of sophistication or self-knowledge. But Thackeray's prose demands that readers trust the showman, the writer, as a consummate practitioner in 'sleight of tongue', because, for his part, the author has trusted the reader implicitly to retain control over his or her own credulity and skepticism. Thackeray does not, for all his pretended intrusions and explanations and instructions, actually spell it out for the reader. He expects to be understood as an ironist.

Readers who view Thackeray as a weak, occasionally inept writer who reached, perhaps, a few peaks of creative genius but who also wallowed in the depths of mundane hackwork, tend not to trust the writer's voice. They will identify each deviance from expectation more quickly as an authorial failing than a controlled nuance demanding dexterity in the reader. In his early writings, Thackeray resorted to editorial footnotes – a kind of 'voice-over effect' – to explain some of his subtle ventriloquist efforts. *Catherine* and *Barry Lyndon* have frequently been remarked as failures of voice whose footnotes showed a faltering authorial hand. Many in Thackeray's early public, and indeed now, did not 'know' the speaker or trust the voice to be fluent and humorous and thus they failed to reach the reading that is subtle, sure and revealing.

Even in *Pendennis* the narrator interrupts himself to 'instruct' the reader on the limitations of the narrator's knowledge and on the readers' responsibilities to judge for themselves: 'We are not pledging ourselves,' the narrator protests, 'for the correctness of [Arthur's] opinions, which readers will please to consider are delivered dramatically, the writer being no more answerable for them, than for the sentiments uttered by any other character of the story: our endeavour is merely to follow out, in its progress, the development of the mind of a worldly and selfish, but not ungenerous or unkind or truth-avoiding man.'[9] Is this sort of instruction necessary because Thackeray fears readers wish to be told explicitly what to think?

How can a writer of Thackeray's temperament and caution – with an ability to see more than one side to every issue – how can such a writer possibly tell readers explicitly what to think? Besides, as a humorist, Thackeray wants to be able to pretend to tell us what to think by asserting at times the very thing he wishes us to question. This is very tricky business. The next sentence following the one just quoted says, 'And it will be seen that the lamentable stage to which his [Arthur's] logic at present has brought him, is one of general scepticism and sneering acquiescence in the world as it is; or if you like so to call it, a belief qualified with scorn in all things extant.' It is the adjective 'lamentable' which seems to say the narrator is telling us what to think immediately after telling us that as a writer he is not telling us what to think. And the alternative to a state of 'general scepticism' is 'belief qualified with scorn', offered as the way the reader might put it.

Thackeray himself was 'guilty' of admiring 'general scepticism' and recognized his own 'belief qualified with scorn' as a natural and honest intellectual stance. But here he pretends that readers would not agree. And he is probably right. Victorians are frequently portrayed as anxious about their beliefs, repudiating disbelief, fearing that qualifications on belief might undermine security. So Thackeray puts his views in the mouth of Arthur (Pen) Pendennis, distances himself from them, warns the reader to judge for himself, suggests a critical stance for the reader to adopt. And then, in a totally different tack of his own, Thackeray the writer undermines Pendennis the narrator's position by showing 17 pages later that Pen is nursing this philosophical stance because it helps him to win and accept the woman, the money and the honors offered him by his worldly uncle. 'Ah well,' one can almost hear the voice of Thackeray muttering in the background, 'Who is there whose position is *not* so constructed and massaged and developed? Who is there who has not found self-satisfaction in the set of beliefs professed, whatever the 'real' motive for holding them?'. What he actually wrote was:

> When a man is tempted to do a tempting thing, he can find a hundred ingenious reasons for gratifying his liking; and Arthur thought very much that he would like to be in Parliament, and that he would like to distinguish himself there, and that he need not care much what side he took, as there was falsehood and truth on every side. And on this and on other matters he thought he would compromise with his conscience, and that Sadduceeism was a very convenient and good-humoured profession of faith.

Pendennis is no less a self-deceiver than his almost father-in-law, Francis Clavering, who must pay off his wife's first husband to keep him quiet. And Pendennis briefly conducts his life in the hope of benefiting from the same fortune that sustains the thoroughly disreputable Francis.

The narratorial voice or voices may well have been the prime strategy with which Thackeray negotiated the most practical difficulty of a writer in his position: one who depended on his pen for a livelihood but whose social and moral visions differed from those of a majority of his potential readers. Thackeray once confided in the atheist writer John Mitchell that he was determined 'not to martyrize himself with his public for the sake of his views', and yet Thackeray was also too committed to 'the truth as I see it' to compromise himself with the public. And so he raises questions and toys with them and pretends to have certain attitudes toward them, all the while undermining the reader's conventional surety and yet not insisting that the reader adopt any of the narrator's views. Few writers on Thackeray have credited his self-subversive prose, increasingly disdainful of simple answers, as a deliberate strategy serving a serious philosophical bent. The easier judgment is to believe his fictive powers failed him – a position that requires belief in a late resurgence of those powers in *Denis Duval*, the novel cut off unfinished at his death. That is to say, readers who preferred the more concrete, less reflective, narrative style of his early works find a return to it in his last novel. Thackeray had not lost his ability to do that sort of thing; he had chosen to follow an inclination toward which, he came to realize, many readers were disinclined.

It is not likely that anyone will rehabilitate Thackeray's later works in the minds of young or casual readers, but the seeds of 'failure' in those works can be read in the successes of the early works, whose primary attraction for most readers lies in their keenly satiric view of society rather than in their self-mockery or subtle probing of self-consciousness. But Thackeray is a humourist not a satirist.[10] The difference between satire and humor is as profound as the difference between the outside view and the inside view. The satirist exposes and prods from external viewpoints, using imposed moral and aesthetic judgments. The result is raucous laughter and bitter distrust of 'the other' who is the object of the satiric gaze. The humorist, on the other hand, explores and probes from within, explaining and making plausible every foible and flaw, and observing, with a wry grin, the ulterior motives behind every public act by tracing the negotiations each individual conducts between ethics and self-forgiveness and self-deceptions. The result is a sad laughter at our own shortcomings and a cautious distrust of 'the self' who is the object of the humorous insight. The humorist demonstrates that the differences between heroes and scoundrels and ourselves are as unstable as quicksilver. This view is compatible with the immortal Pogo's observation: 'We have met the enemy and it is us.'

The primary characteristic of Thackeray's vision is its distrust of human judgment, resulting in a profound compassion for 'sinners' and a deep suspicion of dogma and certainty, which prevented him from adopting for long any of the radical or righteous positions required in order to maintain satire. One result has been Thackeray's inability to maintain the admiration of dogmatic or insecure readers looking for uplifting, high-minded fiction, depicting the world as it ought to be – with evil always punished and good rewarded in the end. Similarly, indignant persons seeking an author who confirms their notion that the world is filled primarily by villains whom they love to hate will be disappointed by Thackeray's frequent discovery of human qualities in vain and hypocritical but not usually profoundly evil characters.

It is said, by those who apparently lack confidence in the young, that one must be at least forty to really appreciate Thackeray. If one supposes that satiric, judgmental laughter appeals to the young more than the supposedly wiser, mild laughter of self-detection – if one supposes that the young lack the patience it may take to realize the complexities of life that deny us the pleasure of admiring heroes and hating villains – then perhaps there is an element of truth in this snobbery of older readers. But it could be said with equal injustice that older readers tend to shy away from writers who expose and explode the small comforting lies of conventional living. By this view it would take the vigor of youth to appreciate Thackeray's works.

For readers wanting the satisfying surety and direction of novelists like Dickens, Eliot or Trollope, Thackeray's endless deferral of certainty and slowness to form final judgments can easily be mistaken for vacillation or failure of nerve. Even those who greatly admire Thackeray may find they are as mistaken in their admiration as Charlotte Brontë was. In the preface to the second edition of *Jane Eyre*, she proclaimed Thackeray 'the greatest social regenerator of his age', conjuring a Carlylean vision of the hero as man of letters, but she was disappointed upon meeting him to find what to her steady gaze and narrow experience was a weak man with internal contradictions. Thomas Carlyle who knew him and his daughters and who liked him, also lamented what he took to be Thackeray's weakness as a person. Many readers have begun by admiring the clarity with which Thackeray exposed the vanities and hypocrisies that debilitate society and that hurt even those who succeed in their deceptions; but then they have become disappointed by Thackeray's lack of a positive agenda for reform. Thackeray, they conclude, may have been a keen observer of society's flaws, but he was no regenerator of the age, no hero as man of letters. Indeed, he was not, nor did he try to be. His genius lies not with the reformers of society but with the reformers of language and vision – an altogether greater undertaking.

Persons of strongly passionate views, like those whose simple understanding of others is based on too small an experience of life or too narrow a view of it, often make mistakes concerning the character of those who distrust certainty; for the ability to see both sides of an argument seems a rare gift, undervalued in the Victorian age, as perhaps also in ours. Even the novelist Anthony Trollope who is often mistakenly seen as Thackeray's closest and greatest imitator, failed utterly to understand and appreciate Thackeray's moral vision. Trollope, too, portrays the good in his evil characters and the weaknesses of his 'heroes and heroines', and he begs the reader from time to time to postpone judgment of his characters, but it is because he knows them so well and is sure of the end and knows that he risks nothing, for the moment, in being fair. Thackeray, by contrast, defers judgment because, unlike the omniscient narrator of most Victorian fictions, he does not know the end and does not trust what he knows; he waits to find out rather than to reveal later something he already knows.

This *Literary Life of Thackeray* explores the view that the reader's portrait of the author influences the understanding of and appreciation for the literary texts, that the reader's sense of the character and voice of the one speaking determines how he or she takes what is said. I try to examine Thackeray's literary life in his personal life and in his fiction, reviews, essays and travel books, but I pursue the various arguments in these areas only far enough to establish the plausibility and critical value of the view. I have tried to include enough of the political, social, literary, artistic, religious and commercial life of Thackeray and his contemporaries to show the ways in which his life and literary output were both conventional and innovative.

Among the issues most recently opened by criticism of Thackeray's works are his attitudes toward gender, toward the position of women in the marriage market, and toward race, slavery and non-Anglos – particularly Frenchmen, Jews and Mediterranean Orientals. One could say that his fiction constitutes an analysis of the human pecking order. Thackeray's religious and philosophical views have been treated briefly by Geoffrey Tillotson in *A View of Victorian Literature* and best by Robert Colby in *Thackeray: A Canvass of Humanity*, but these areas remain otherwise virtually unexplored; yet I believe that a rich and sympathetic response to his narrative techniques derives from an understanding of his philosophical questionings and his religious agnosticism. A key to the importance of his determined deferral of judgment is found in *The Newcomes*: 'the wicked are wicked no doubt, and they go astray and they fall, and they come by their deserts: but who can measure the mischief which the very virtuous do?'. The biblical cadence combined with a definitely nonbiblical sentiment sharpens the bite of this idea. The fear of doing evil by trying to do good disarmed Thackeray's satire, his ire and his self-promotion. What he offers instead is infinitely more important, satisfying and disturbing – as I hope will become clear as we progress.

Thackeray was very conscious, from youth until death, of the importance both in real life and in fiction of the creation of self-portraits. In a letter home, written soon after he had abandoned college and while he was 'looking about himself' during a half-year's sojourn in Weimar, Germany, the young Thackeray complained:

> Your letters always make me sorrowful, dearest Mother, for there seems some hidden cause of dissatisfaction, some distrust which you do not confess & cannot conceal & for which on looking into myself I can find no grounds or reason – Idleness irresolution & extravagance are charges wh. have been long laid against me, & to which I know I am still but too open – but I can say that tho' still idle & extravagant I am not so much so as when in England, for here I have more inducement to industry & less temptation to expense.[11]

The difference between his mother's apparent view of him and his own leads to very different judgments. Of course here we have only the young Thackeray's view, but it rings true to many youths whose sense is that the mother hovers overbearingly, expecting the young to fulfill parental rather than personal goals. Thackeray certainly felt that, for he continued:

> You seem to take it so much to heart, that I gave up trying for Academical honors – perhaps Mother I was too young to form opinions but I did form them – & these told me that there was little use in studying what could after a certain point be of no earthly use to me… that three years of industrious waste of time might obtain for me mediocre honours wh. I did not value at a straw[. I]s it because I have unfortunately fallen into this state of thinking that you are so dissatisfied with me[?] … Mother mother would it not have been better to have consulted my inclinations & have fostered them than to have persevered in a system which was determined on long before the object of it had manifested any talents or desires for or against it. … I know that the system you pursued you considered was the best… but I who was the object of it because now I am old enough to think & to act a little for myself am *thought* idle & ungrateful – because I consider it unsuited to me, & do what I can to pursue a different one –[12]

The battle of wills here revealed was to continue through his entire life. The mother whom he loved and resisted died one year after the son. But his fiction and his letters are informed by his sensitivity to the private view, privileged by self knowledge and different from the external view, whether held by loving but domineering and therefore often disappointed parents or by the bitterest of enemies, including one's former friends. Two and a half years before he died, writing to his friend, the Revd Whitwell Elwin, Thackeray meditated a moral on the occasion of his having been blackballed from membership in the Literary Club:

> All people dont like me as you do. I think sometimes I am deservedly unpopular and in some cases I rather like it. Why should I want to be liked by Jack and Tom? ... I know the Thackeray that those fellows have imagined to themselves [is] a very selfish heartless artful morose and designing man –[13]

Indeed, each reader's assessment of Thackeray's writings is dependent upon the portrait from which emerges the writer's voice in the re-creative imagination of the reader. This book is written to influence the portrait of Thackeray which readers will create and take to Thackeray's writings. I hope that the character of Thackeray drawn in this book will help account for all the voices in his works, for Thackeray is among the most accomplished ventriloquists to have written the Queen's English. And his ventriloquism is not merely the showman's tricks to entertain a passing crowd. The voices and the roles which call them forth are endemic to Thackeray's views of society, of men and women, and of the writer's responsibilities to his vision and to his audiences. A simple mistake about the author or the narrator will cause the reader to misconstrue the voice, and hence the meaning, effect, and value of the prose.

In order to recognize the voice of a character who is speaking in a particular tone and with a particular style that provides evidence of a particular social, moral, political or aesthetic stance, the reader must develop a sense of the range of possibilities with which a given writer can be credited. If one is unwilling to grant the writer a particular voice, one will dismiss approximations to it as mistakes or inconsistencies.

Even when we know the writer's range of technique, we might still fail to grant his range of vision. Thackeray's movement through several social ranks, his view of social differences, when known to us, will affect our sense of what he is showing, what he is criticizing, who and what he values. Similarly, his religious experiences and responses, his philosophical readings and meditations, his understanding of what can and cannot be known but might be believed will indicate to readers the range of meanings available both for his characters and for the central informing intelligence of his works. Thackeray's experiences and responses to aesthetic objects – paintings, music, plays, operas, sculpture and particularly novels, essays and short fictions by other writers – shaped his own notions of what is genuine and what is sham in appeals to emotional and aesthetic senses. The ironist depends on readers who share external standards of social, political, and moral right, by which the ironic rhetoric and presentation of events is judged. Without such shared standards, the rhetoric of irony is confusing or highly susceptible to misunderstanding, for the ironist's technique is to say what is meant by saying what is not meant.

It is the conclusion of this study that Thackeray's range in technique and vision was great and ample to support a nuanced and sophisticated response to his writings. It is more likely that what we do not like in Thackeray's writings is what we do not understand than that it was ill-conceived or badly represented.

# 2
# Youth and Family

William Thackeray was born into established financial and social expectations that shaped his youthful aspirations and sense of self-worth. Of a solid family tree generously represented with professional educators, physicians, clergymen and company officials, he was welcome in high middle-class and lower upper-class circles, with personal wealth that gave him the freedom to do well or merely to dilly-dally in school or in a profession. He was a public school boy,[14] comfortable in income, and destined to a life driven by pursuit of desires – a young man, in short, with all the makings of a George Osborne in *Vanity Fair*: a self-satisfied dandy, expecting the world to open itself for his superior talents. And yet, like Georgie while still in Chiswick School, young Thackeray did not stand out as obnoxious in any way. John Fredrick Boyes, a son in the family with whom Thackeray boarded when he became a day boy at Charterhouse, noted that Thackeray was stout but not tall (he grew six inches during an illness in the summer he finished school) and had 'dark curling hair, and a quick, intelligent eye, ever twinkling with humour, and *good* humour ... so jovial, so healthy, and so sedentary'.[15] He developed close and important friendships in school and college, showed an early talent for writing and for drawing comic sketches, and in college developed ways of enjoying himself and entertaining friends that brought gray hairs to his mother's head.

Thackeray was born on 18 July 1811 in Calcutta, India, where his father, Richmond Thackeray, a second son who had to make his own way in the world, went to seek his fortune. By the time young

William arrived, Richmond had amassed a respectable estate, dying when William was four, and leaving his wealth primarily to his only son, but including small legacies for his Indian mistress and illegitimate daughter. Although Thackeray's mother, Anne Becher, became rather straightlaced and, Thackeray thought, worried excessively about appearances and morals, there were interesting and traumatic episodes of intergenerational conflict in her own and her mother's histories.

When William's mother Anne was still a small child, her mother, Harriet Becher, abandoned her husband and daughters to elope with a Captain Charles Christie, with whom she lived, apparently unwed, until his death. She then married Captain Edward William Butler of the Bengal Artillery in October 1806, by which time Mr Becher, her first and, to that point, only legal husband, had died. Anne Becher was reared, not by her wayward mother, but by her paternal grandmother, also named Anne Becher, a woman of severe evangelical beliefs, who cultivated ambitions for her granddaughter – specifically, a marriage of wealth and position. Unfortunately, when the time came for Anne to fall in love, she chose Henry Carmichael-Smyth, an ensign of small expectations. Her grandmother of course objected to the connection, restricted the girl to her bedroom, cajoled her, and finally lied, telling Anne that the young man had died. Grandmother Becher returned all the love letters to Carmichael-Smyth, telling him that Anne no longer cared for him. The prematurely bereaved Anne was sent to India along with her sister Harriet and her mother, now restored to the fold of the respectable by three years of marriage to Captain Butler.

Versions of this story of betrayals and parental manipulations show up over and over in Thackeray's fiction. Among the more pointed retellings is the account of Arthur Pendennis's first love and the ostensible real-life parallel upon which Thackeray may have based it. Arthur, better known as Pen, falls for a countrytown actress, Emily Fotheringay, a woman completely inappropriate for him from his family's point of view: she was 10 years his senior, completely uneducated, poor, and following a disreputable profession, and she was the daughter of a garrulous Irish ne'er-do-well drunk. Because Pen's father had died, his mother invited his uncle, Major Arthur Pendennis, to come and deal with the situation. Of course, Pen, blinded by love to all the impediments to his happiness, is incensed at the thought of parental, or in this case avuncular, interference in his personal affairs.

It is alleged that Thackeray, just before writing the opening chapters of *Pendennis*, heard the story of a real-life case of parental manipulation and betrayal, not unlike the story of his mother's first love, though with an even less happy ending. Thackeray's daughter recorded the story:

> there was a somewhat autocratic father and a romantic young son who had lost his heart to the housemaid and determined to marry her. The father made the young man give his word of honour that he would not marry clandestinely, and then having dismissed him rang the bell for the butler. To the butler this Major Pendennis said, 'Morgan' (or whatever his name was), 'I wish you to retire from my service, but I will give £200 in bank-notes if you will marry the housemaid before twelve o'clock tomorrow.' The butler said, 'Certainly, sir,' and the young man next morning was told of that which had occurred. As far as I remember a melancholy and sensational event immediately followed; for the poor young fellow was so overwhelmed that he rushed out and distractedly blew his brains out on the Downs behind the house, and the butler meanwhile, having changed his £200, sent a message to say that he had omitted to mention that he had a wife already, and that this would doubtless invalidate the ceremony he had just gone through with the housemaid.[16]

In Arthur Pendennis's case, his uncle dealt not autocratically nor essentially dishonestly but with craft, persuading Arthur to think himself far too good to throw himself away and to think upon what folks in *real* society, to which Arthur *really* belonged, would think of such a connection. In the end Arthur merely rides his horse nearly to death on the Downs behind the house. The young man recovers and is able to lose his heart or to pretend to lose it several more times. But the parallel to the novelist's mother's early experience is inescapable, showing either that parental disapproval of an offspring's first choice in love is nearly universal or that Thackeray's knowledge of his mother's story made him especially sensitive to this potential source of intergenerational friction.

Young Anne Becher was beautiful and soon made noticeable inroads in Calcutta's Anglo-Indian social circles, where Richmond

Thackeray joined many other suitors seeking her attentions. Like many East India officials posted far from home as young bachelors to gain wealth before marriage, Richmond had previously contented his cravings for female companionship with an Indian mistress by whom he had a daughter named Sarah. Anne and her sister Harriet, like many young ladies before them, had come into a country where women were at a premium, so to speak, and almost none lacked suitors. It was a country in which no one objected or thought it unusual when Richmond made other arrangements for his temporary native liaison in order to pay court to Anne Becher. He prevailed and they married in 1810. Richmond Thackeray was on the rise; Anne Becher was his reward.

Within a year, a son was born, and five months later Richmond was promoted to the post of collector of the House Tax at Calcutta and of the Twenty-four Pergunnahs, south of Calcutta, posts with substantial incomes and with opportunities for and obligations to entertain widely. In the second year of his marriage, Richmond brought a new friend home to dine, Captain Henry Carmichael-Smyth, Anne's first and presumed 'dead' love. We can only guess at the recognition scene. Was it a case of suppressed emotions and polite greetings or an outburst and hasty retraction? Had time healed the wounds and changed attitudes? Did someone faint? Whatever the case, Mrs Fuller (the couple's great granddaughter) writes, 'After a while the situation became so impossible that Richmond Thackeray had to be told; he listened gravely, said little, but was never the same to Anne again.'[17] The quotation has the ring of family history, seeming to explain with ambiguous phrases (what did that last 'was never the same' really mean?), rather than ringing true to human nature. How could Richmond from the start have failed to notice that he was introducing old acquaintances? And, since nothing had been allowed to pass between the Henry and Anne in England, what was there, other than lost hopes, to regret? It is difficult to imagine what the two old lovers had to tell Richmond to which he would listen gravely. It is not likely that they confessed a continued or renewed love, now rendered illicit by Anne's marriage to Richmond. Even if there had been a 'deeper relationship' between the separated lovers, it does not seem likely that they would have felt compelled by honor to confess it to the husband; for they had not betrayed anyone in their actions. Indeed, they were the ones betrayed. So, it seems unlikely that the granddaughter's account is accurate. To us, in an age believing itself to be more open about such matters, it would not have been unusual for Richmond, himself possessor of a prior mistress and daughter, to hold his wife to a different standard. Perhaps he thought that because the break between them had been accomplished by falsity, its renewal was inevitable; perhaps in Richmond's mind Anne still loved Henry.

Be that as it may, Anne and Henry stayed apart, and young William's first five years passed in a house of apparent harmony and wealth, surrounded by native house servants and a mother and aunt who had little else to do than to play with the child and pamper his wishes. The young boy had his own native servant, a youngster whose job was to do whatever young Thackeray asked. Soon, however, Fate intervened on behalf of the old lovers, for Richmond Thackeray died in September of 1815, within three years of the old lovers' reunion, leaving an estate worth £17 000. Just over two years later, in November 1817, Anne and Henry were wed. But first, following the customs of the English in India, the widow sent her only son 'home' to begin his education in England and to avoid the threat of childhood diseases in a foreign climate.

Richmond's will suggests by its ordinariness and its directness that he was an honorable man who did not bear grudges beyond the grave. His wife had a lifetime annuity of £450 a year; he left £100 annuities each to his sister Augusta, his son William, and his illegitimate daughter Sarah, and he left simple amounts of £30 to Sarah's mother and an old servant. The bulk of the estate would belong to young William on his 21st birthday. In the meantime, in November 1816, the five-year-old boy was dispatched to England for his own good. He would see his mother again, married to a stranger, when the couple returned to England in 1819.

The righteous, wicked old grandmother, Anne Becher the elder, by the way, having fulfilled as best she could the role of defender of the family aspirations, can hardly be said to have failed utterly, for though the lovers she separated had now returned conjoined, a small fortune had meanwhile been acquired, and, perhaps as a result of his earlier disappointment, Henry Carmichael-Smyth turned out to be both interesting and substantial. Young William came to know his great grandmother, Anne Becher, when he spent the summer of 1818 at her home. He came to know his grandmother, Mrs Butler, fairly well and to benefit from her meager generosity and suffer from her increasing cantankerousness when he stayed with her in Paris, in his days as a would-be painter, and again when she lived with him briefly in 1840–41 and 1847, the year she died. There seems to be more than just a bit of her character, though none of her financial condition, in Miss Crawley in *Vanity Fair*.

On his journey to England young Thackeray was accompanied by a friend of the family, by his cousin Richmond Shakespeare who was being sent home on the same mission, and by a native servant named Lawrence Barlow. Every biographer has found it necessary to mention that when the ship stopped at St Helena, Barlow took Thackeray to peep over a wall at a man walking in a garden; 'that is Bonaparte!' said the servant, 'He eats three sheep every day, and all the little children he can lay hands on!'[18] or so the novelist recalled 38 years later in a lecture on George III. Arriving 'home', William's first stop was a brief stay with his aunt Charlotte Sarah (Richmond's sister) and her husband John Ritchie in the summer of 1817 before attending with his cousin Richmond Shakespeare a school 'of which our deluded parents had heard a favourable report, but which was governed by a horrible little tyrant, who made our young lives so miserable that I remember kneeling by my little bed of a night, and saying, "Pray God, I may dream of my mother!"'.[19]

The emotions of early separation from his mother, translation from a pampered family setting to a stringent boarding-school life, and the real or imagined frightfulness of parental abandonment shows up in the childhood feelings and experiences of several of Thackeray's fictional characters, especially Henry Esmond, who was left an orphan for the second time and in a big house about to be occupied by strangers. These sad emotions are also felt by young William Dobbin in *Vanity Fair* who forgot his real woes in the delights of the *Arabian Nights*, and by the 'lazy idle boy' of the *Roundabout Papers* whose love of books had more to do with escape than any love of learning, and by many other youngsters in Thackeray's fiction. He may have started life as a pampered mother's darling, but Thackeray clearly understood and sympathized with childhood loneliness and fear.

Some of Thackeray's biographers have tried to imagine the young boy's feelings about his step-father, Major Carmichael-Smyth. In the fully understandable absence of evidence one way or the other, they construct Oedipal objections to the father figure, perhaps because of the obvious love expressed in his affectionate letters to his mother all his life. Whatever his feelings might have been as a child, Thackeray developed a respect and affection for the Major who proved to be a very supportive force in his life. When Thackeray's fortune was lost in Indian bank failures, the Major came to his rescue in a journalism venture whose failure in turn seriously affected the Major's finances.

After the first unfortunate school, Thackeray spent four years attending a boarding school at Chiswick after which he enrolled at the ancient and famous but not much more humane Charterhouse School, where he spent the next six years. Summers he spent at first with his paternal grandmother who lived in an Anglo-Indian enclave and hotbed of evangelical fervor at Fareham. Although his own memories of India do not appear much in his works, he drew readily on the Indian connections of Fareham's returned East India men in portraits of Jos in *Vanity Fair*, Major Pendennis in *Pendennis*, and Colonel Newcome in *The Newcomes*. Thackeray set only one of his works in India, *The Tremendous Adventures of Major Gahagan* (1838), in which the exaggerated recollections of Gahagan must have drawn on many such tales told at Fareham. When his mother and Major Carmichael-Smyth returned in 1819, he summered with them at Addiscombe, near Croydon, until 1825, when they moved to a house named Larkbeare near Ottery St Mary and Exeter. This latter setting became the terrain of Arthur Pendennis's youth, transformed into Clavering and Chatteris. The rector of nearby Clyst Hydon, the Reverend Francis Huyshe, became a close family friend and was probably the model for Dr Portman in *Pendennis*.

Though Thackeray ended in better schools than his first one at Southampton, his recollections of school tyrannies and the terrors of schoolboyhood show up repeatedly in his fiction. His portraits of teachers in various works – Miss Tickletoby, Dr Birch and Dr Swishtail, whose names are indicative of their methods – and his descriptions of Slaughterhouse, Blackfriars, Greyfriars and Whitefriars schools suggest that flogging and fagging were the primary agents of instruction. One of the first orders issued to him by an upperclassman upon his arrival at Charterhouse was to 'frig me'. Of course, there is no record of whether he filled the order, but public school reminiscences by others show the practice was not unusual. The place is described in *Vanity Fair* under the name Whitefriars as a place of ancient torture:

> It had been a Cistercian Convent in old days, when the Smithfield, which is contiguous to it, was a tournament ground. Obstinate heretics used to be brought thither convenient for burning hard by. Harry VIII, the Defender of the Faith, seized upon the monastery and its possessions, and hanged and tortured some of the monks who could not accommodate themselves to the pace of his reform. Finally, a great merchant bought the house and land adjoining, in which, and with the help of other wealthy endowments of land and money, he established a famous foundation hospital for old men and children. An extern school grew round the old almost monastic foundation, which subsists still with its middle-age costume and usages: and all Cistercians pray that it may long flourish.[20]

Why Thackeray's attitude toward the brutalities of that system mellowed as he grew older is something of a mystery. Did he grow insensitive to the pain, or did he come to attribute some of his own strength of character to the hardships of youth? Were there enough good times and friendships made to mitigate the evils of the place? His earlier recollections were that he had been 'licked into indolence', 'abused into sulkiness' and 'bullied into despair'.[21] And yet, the letters he wrote home from Southampton and Chiswick do not betray the misery of the schoolboys portrayed in Thackeray's fiction. Perhaps the censoring eyes of proctors and schoolmasters prevented such revelations. Be that as it may, the narratorial voice in *Vanity Fair* interrupts Cuff beating little Georgie Osborne's hand with a wicket stump to remark in an aside to the reader, 'Don't be horrified, ladies, every boy at a public school has done it. Your children will so do and be done by in all probability – Down came the wicket again ...'.[22] Of course, there is great satisfaction in the drubbing Cuff got from Dobbin in consequence of this little episode, but Thackeray seems not only to be describing a real scene of childhood brutality realistically but he also seems to have conceded that nothing can or should be done about it. The evils of the system, perhaps, form the obstacle course that strengthens character. The fact that it did not strengthen George Osborne's character belies the point.

There is good reason, according to the recollections of various former students, to believe that whatever learning took place under Dr Russell's headmastering at Charterhouse was incidental to the moral debauchery, corruption and violence that seems to have prevailed there, as at other public schools.[23]

William's natural abilities caused him to rise through the academic ranks respectably, though he seems, like Arthur Pendennis, to have preferred a reading course of his own devising over the assigned one. Of stories and histories he could not get enough; it was the parsing, translating and memorizing that made him impatient. He covered the margins and endpapers of his school texts with drawings that showed an unusual talent for comic figures. Thackeray was unable to take a very active role in games, in part because of his poor eyesight and, perhaps, because he was naturally sedentary. Had he had spectacles, they would have prevented the rougher sports. One sporting event in which he did participate, however, left him with a broken nose – a fist fight with his friend George Venables, provoked apparently by no other motive than for the amusement of the other boys.[24]

Rising to the first form in his last year at Charterhouse, where upperclassmen did much of the lower form teaching (because it saved the school money), Thackeray had the misfortune of receiving 'instruction' directly from Dr Russell, about whom Thackeray wrote home in words facetious ('I have got four hours of delightful Doctor Russell to day before me, is it not felicitous? Every day he begins at me. Thackeray Thackeray! you are an idle profligate shuffling boy, ... ') and plaintive ('Doctor Russell is treating me every day with such manifest unkindness and injustice, that I really can scarcely bear it: It is so hard when you endeavour to work hard, to find your attempts nipped in the bud – if I ever get a respectable place in my form, he is sure to bring me down again; to day there was such a flagrant instance of it, that it was the general talk of the school – I wish I could take leave of him tomorrow – He will have this to satisfy himself with, that he has thrown every possible object in my way to prevent my exerting myself ... ').[25] Thackeray's parodies of Russell began while in school and show up in much of his fiction. When Arthur Pendennis did not know his Horace or could not construe a Greek play, the Doctor at Greyfriars 'said that that boy Pendennis was a disgrace to the school, a candidate for ruin in this world, and perdition in the next; a profligate who would most likely bring his venerable father to ruin and his mother to a dishonoured grave'. And echoing Thackeray's letter home about Dr Russell, Pen's teacher ranted, 'Pendennis, sir, ... your idleness is incorrigible and your stupidity beyond example. You are a disgrace to your school and to your family, and I have no doubt will prove so in after-life to your country.'[26]

Thackeray's formal education included little mathematics, and its rote approach to classics did little for the understanding. But Thackeray read constantly, and he had a painter's (or at least a caricaturist's) eye for the people and places surrounding him. His sense of class distinctions in English society also developed some complexity at Charterhouse; for though the public schools mixed the sons of the very wealthy with a few of those from lesser families, public school boys were keenly aware of their membership in a community separate from all others. A tongue-in-cheek passage in *Vanity Fair* describes the mixed bag found in the fictional Charterhouse, renamed Whitefriars:

> some of the richest people did not disdain it; and not only great men's relations, but great men themselves, sent their sons to profit by the chance [to get an education for nothing, and a future livelihood and profession assured] – Right Rev. Prelates sent their own kinsmen or the sons of their clergy, while, on the other hand, some great noblemen did not disdain to patronise the children of their confidential servants, – so that a lad entering this establishment had every variety of youthful society wherewith to mingle.[27]

But this apparent 'democracy' of backgrounds disappears in the homogeneity of the products. The education may not have been much, but the experience and the friendships formed there made all the difference. There is more than a little truth in the notion that the *Book of Snobs* was 'written by one of them'; for though Thackeray was able to see and depict the pretensions and overreaching of English snobbism, he never 'forgot his place' or the codes learned in public school that separated him from the less privileged.

Thackeray left Charterhouse in April 1828 to spend the summer at Larkbeare preparing for college in the autumn, but he fell seriously ill of a fever that laid him up for several months. His slow recovery and the idleness of the summer and autumn probably, in many ways, was similar to the idle months Pendennis spent at Fairoaks upon leaving school, when he fell in love with the Fotheringay, wrote his first poems for the newspaper, fished the local stream, galloped his horse upon the Downs and patronized his half sister, Laura. Except that in Thackeray's case, the poems in the newspaper were ironic, not sentimental, the actress he mooned over was Mrs Yates, whom he had seen in London while still in school, and little Laura was actually his orphan cousin Mary Graham, who had lived with the Carmichael-Smyths since 1820.

The upshot of his illness was that Thackeray did not go to Cambridge, until February 1829, giving his step-father, though he was not himself a college man, eight months to 'coach' Thackeray in maths and the classics. Carmichael-Smyth, whom Thackeray called 'Father' or 'PA', accompanied him to Cambridge to settle him into Isaac Newton's old room in Trinity College.

In trying to answer the questions, who was Thackeray? whose is the voice that will speak in his novels? how will our portrait of Thackeray affect how we take what he says? one is tempted to try to understand the young Thackeray by comparing him with the portraits of some of his characters into whom he might have put his own understanding of who he had been or might have been in his own youth. The parallel most frequently drawn by biographers is with Arthur Pendennis, a comparison Thackeray himself encouraged. This parallel, developed in more detail in future chapters, is usually taken to be exculpatory or even flattering to Thackeray, though it strikes me as somewhat ambiguous, as will be explained. Charlotte Brontë, however, insisted that the real parallel was with George Warrington – not the one in *The Virginians* but the one in *The History of Pendennis* who was a more intelligent and serious person. Brontë meant it as a compliment for she approved of Warrington's serious and rather judgmental intelligence, and she was rather disappointed when she detected traces of Pendennis or worse in Thackeray's facetious, self-deprecating humor. Henry Esmond is also offered by some biographers and critics as an alter ego for the author because of his reflective nature and his ability to detect hidden motives, sometimes even in himself.

Each of these analogues with Thackerayan heroes is worth exploring, but a darker picture emerges if one suggests George Osborne whom Becky Sharp describes with some justice as 'that selfish humbug, that low-bred cockney-dandy, that padded booby, who had neither wit, nor manners, nor heart'.[28] One can almost hear Thackeray, as he developed Osborne's character, saying, 'There but for the grace of God go I.' George, of course, saw himself in a different light: he was an only son who was to inherit his rich but low-bred father's estate without having to work at his father's or any other trade; he had the education, the looks, the confidence, the expectations of wealth and the social graces that made him believe other men envied him and any woman who got him would be lucky indeed; he would be king of his household and do as he pleased.

*Figure 2.1* Vignette of George Osborne as the Letter I, *Vanity Fair*, 123

This dark portrait of Thackeray is somewhat exaggerated, but the seeds of dandyism, of an attitude of superiority, and of a lack of appreciation for the feelings and strengths of women can be seen in Thackeray's life from 17 to 29. The process by which he came to recognize these aspects of himself and to purge them left him with the ability to see and understand characters like George Osborne, Barry Lyndon, and Barnes Newcome – fictional characters who never gain self-awareness – or like Sam Titmarsh (of the *Great Hoggarty Diamond*) and Arthur Pendennis, who were like them until a series of personal set-backs slowly brought them to self-knowledge and change.

The point of this invitation to see Thackeray's own developing character in the shadows cast by some of his darker male characters is to point to the ordinariness of these unpleasant qualities in the general population of Thackeray's schoolboy friends and acquaintances and in the population of his books. The list of insensitive, male chauvinists in his books is nearly endless, including all the Lords Castlewood, Lords Hamilton and Mohun (in different ways) in *Henry Esmond*, Henry and George Warrington and the Castlewoods and Tushers in *The Virginians*, the older Osborne and Lord Steyne and Jos in *Vanity Fair*. These men were not criminals, nor were they without honor and even acclaim. But Thackeray shows them from the point of view of women, from whom their essential insensitivity is not hidden, even when the women's dependence upon them or devoted loyalty to them is also present.

*Figure 2.2* Self-portrait as the Letter I for 'Out of Town', *Punch*, 17 (1849), 53

Men's ability – tendency really – to see themselves as deserving egos is not limited to any level of society in Thackeray's fiction. But it can be contended that it took one to know the breed. Young Thackeray was well on his way to becoming an ordinary product of his education. Its main elements consisted of a tender ego nurtured by a loving British mother like Anne Becher Thackeray Carmichael-Smyth who, like Helen Pendennis, taught her son to think well of himself and to expect pampering from his women; training in the tactics of receiving and delivering humiliation, learned through extended hazing by upper-classmen and teachers alike in public school in order to become an initiate in an élite category of persons; and the 'mean admiration of mean things' such as preferment, clothing and the notice of persons higher up on the pecking order. There is nothing unusual about the process or the product – except that in Thackeray's case there was the potential for keen observation, reflection, ironic detachment and recognition that allowed him to see the unpleasant portrait in the mirror as well as in faces met on the street.

And Thackeray had or developed a generosity of spirit and toleration that rejected the equally insensitive, self-righteous reactions of persons like Miss Pinkerton, Mrs Bute Crawley, Dr Portman, Bishop Tusher or even Thomas Newcome, to mention just a few characters capable of extreme injustice in the name of virtue. To a person these 'moral' characters lacked the sense of humor and the comic vision that, in combination with a distrust of certainty, ultimately saved Thackeray from stridence. Thackeray learned to forgive the pecadillos and eccentricities of others – and, truth be told, to forgive himself as well – which is disappointing to many moralists whose inability to note the beam in their own eye does not keep them from pointing accusing fingers at the motes in the eyes of others. But before Thackeray learned his lessons and developed these perspectives, he had great expectations of college and inheritance to blind him to the flaws of his conventional upbringing.

# 3

# Gentleman and Literary Hack

On his father's side, Thackeray's great grandfather was an archdeacon, several great uncles and cousins were physicians, his cousin Elias was a vicar, two cousins filled the posts of Provost and Vice-Provost of King's College, Cambridge, and a cousin by marriage was a Cambridge professor of political economy. It seems natural, then, that his mother should have had high aspirations for her son. Because Thackeray entered college late, his relative, the Vice-Provost, counseled him to forego the exams in the first year. Following that advice would have added a year to his course of study and might have put his mother's expectations within reach. He determined, however, perhaps on the strength of the ego built by his mother, to take the exams, reading for an honours rather than a pass degree. William Whewell, his official tutor, was a scholar much too busy to spend significant time with students. Thackeray's tutor, Henry Fawcett, described him as a ready enough scholar at first. Like Pendennis, he seems to have applied himself with some enthusiasm, his day being devoted to studies and lectures from six in the morning to three every day. But within three months he was describing Fawcett as 'a desperate bore' and complaining that his explanations of trigonometry only obscured that which he thought he already understood.[29] In his second year, Thackeray forsook assiduous attendance at lectures, at first in favor of private reading and then of extra-curricular pursuits. Cambridge distractions included, of course, wine parties and debates and outings.

Nonetheless, Thackeray actually was a reader – even a serious one – of *modern* novels, poems and histories. Shelley's *Revolt of Islam*

*Figure 3.1* Vignette for ch. 19, in which Pendennis goes to college, *Pendennis*, I, 170

was to have been the subject of a *Snob* paper that was never written; and Thackeray intended twice to speak up in debates on the poem, which he described in letters home as a book whose poetry makes one wish to read on but whose sentiments tempt one to throw it in the fire.[30] I suspect the book's sentiments were more attractive than the young man would let on in a letter designed for home consumption. No one has traced in detail or with any persuasiveness the roots of Thackeray's thoughtful lapse from religious orthodoxy – he claimed years later in a letter to his 15-year-old daughter that the evangelical writers he was exposed to in his youth gave him a distaste for dogma – but it cannot be mere chance that Thackeray's mature thought aligned with Shelley's both in its deep compassion and understanding of the wayward and in its rejection of dogma. Thackeray, of course, never adopted Shelley's behavior, never made a public issue of his skepticism, and never flouted social conventions for the purpose of making ideological statements. But it is clear that Shelley made a deep impression on his thinking, perhaps more than on his writing style.

Older writers such as Gibbon, Hume and Smollett (as both historian and novelist) show up in his accounts at the time, and

*Figure 3.2* Vignette for ch. 20, titled 'Rake's Progress', *Pendennis*, I, 183

Thackeray's later published works allude most frequently, after the Bible, Shakespeare and the classics, which would have been standard school fare, to *The Arabian Nights*, Cervantes, Fielding, Byron, Scott, Dumas, Goldsmith, Goethe and household names in 18th-century drama, which made up his voluntary reading. Thackeray frequently cited such reading as an indulgence or temptation – a distraction from legitimate pursuits. But he was inclined to indulge himself, as can be seen in his account of a day of hooky, spent riding and, apparently, watching the gambling at a race course in Newmarket, a few miles from Cambridge. Of course, he wrote home, he would not be going back, and, of course, the ride was very good for him though it left his muscles stiff. It is as if writing home was a way of letting his conscience chide him.

Meanwhile, Thackeray had written poems and a translation for *The Western Luminary*, a Devon newspaper, before heading for college, but at Cambridge he cultivated the friendship of William Williams, editor of the *Snob* and, in the next year, its replacement, the *Gownsman*, student-run papers. Thackeray's first contribution to the *Snob* was his famous 'Timbuctoo', a spoof of the prize poem competition, which Alfred Tennyson won that year. He contributed six more pieces by the end of term in June.

His relatives in Cambridge welcomed Thackeray with open arms, but he found their company staid, and he spent little time with them – we have no record of what they thought of him save one episode preceding the first-year examinations. He was sick for nearly two weeks before the exams, suffering from persistent headache, for which his cousin the physician ordered that leeches be applied to his head. When the 'procedure' apparently succeeded, the doctor gracefully declined payment from his kinsman with the remark, 'What, do you think me a Cannibal?'.[31] Having started in mid-year and having been ill, Thackeray probably should not have taken the exams, but he did – five days of eight hour exams on mathematics and classical authors. Expecting a fifth-class result, he made it to the top of the fourth class 'where clever "non-reading" men were put, as in a limbo'.[32]

In the summer of 1829, following his first half-year at Cambridge and just turning 18, Thackeray chose the company of the *Snob* editor, William Williams, for a vacation in Paris. Having just graduated, Williams was to serve as Thackeray's mathematics coach for the summer, and Thackeray would also learn French and extend his education with Continental experience. But Williams soon abandoned the enterprise, and Thackeray was left to discover museums, artists' studios and Frascati's gambling opportunities for himself. By his account home, his first visit to Frascati's was a brush with evil that taught him the lesson to avoid gambling, but in fact it appears to have whetted his taste for play.

On Thackeray's return to Cambridge in October, distractions continued to outweigh the honours curriculum in maths and classics. It is not known exactly when Thackeray decided that further pursuit of an honours degree was a waste of time, but the decision formed a part of his break for independence from his mother to whom he wrote the next year the letter already quoted in Chapter 1: 'You seem to take it so much to heart ... perhaps Mother I was too young to form opinions but I did form them' and which ended with the plaintive query, is that why 'you are so dissatisfied with me[?]'.[33] He left college for good at the end of his second year, after which his continued but uneasy break from his mother's controlling ideas for him did not quite overcome his desire for her continued love and approval. His mother seemed never able to express disapproval, however, without seeming to withdraw love. Or rather, her standard way to disapprove was to express love's disappointment. The plaintive 'is that why you are so dissatisfied with me' is echoed in the conflicts between Pendennis and his mother, and in the relations between George and Henry Warrington and their mother in *The Virginians*.

Thackeray's second year at Cambridge is remarkable for the friends and mistakes he made. The written evidence for his second-year activities is meager: only four contributions to the *Snob*'s successor the *Gownsman* and two letters home. His circle of acquaintance included important friendships with Henry Alford, John Allen, Henry Nicholson Burrows, Charles Christie, William Hepworth Thompson and John Hailstone – all members of a debating society formed in imitation of the 'Apostles'[34] – the famous group of young Cambrians including Alfred Tennyson (whom Thackeray apparently did not meet until after his college days were over) – and several finding a place in the *Dictionary of National Biography*, the multi-volume record of British biography orchestrated near the end of the century by Leslie Stephen, the man who married Thackeray's daughter Harriet. Other of Thackeray's life-long friendships begun then included those with James Spedding, who became a historian, John Mitchell Kemble, later editor of the *British and Foreign Review*, A.W. Kinglake, who would write travel books and poetry, William Brookfield, a cleric and for 20 years his best friend and Richard Monckton Milnes, Fifth Lord Houghton, book collector and patron of the arts. His best friends in the autumn term were John Allen, who influenced him to affirm his religious beliefs, and Edward Fitzgerald, a shy man who shared Thackeray's love of literature and who influenced him to doubt his beliefs. The former became a famous man of the Church, the latter a famous atheist and translator of *The Rubáiyát of Omar Khayyam*. Fitzgerald graduated in December, leaving the field to Allen, but Thackeray's summer in Paris led him to gravitate to faster men, including Harry Matthews, a bounder who served as the prototype of Bloundel in *Pendennis*. Matthews seems to have led Thackeray on a binge of gambling and drinking in the Lent and Easter terms.

At the Easter break, he announced to his mother he would spend the vacation with a friend named Slingsby in Huntingdonshire, but instead went to Paris with Edward Fitzgerald, an outing about which, he remarked years later, 'my benighted parents never knew anything'.[35] It may have been during this escapade that Thackeray contracted the venereal disease that caused in later life the painful stricture of the urethra, to which he sometime referred in letters explaining bouts of illness as trouble with his 'water works.' What is undeniable is that he spent much of this Paris outing with a woman 10 or 12 years his senior whom he met at a masquerade party. The experience may have been the inspiration for Pendennis's infatuation with Emily Fotheringay, who was 10 years older, and with Fanny Bolton – episodes in which the sexual element, for the sake of mainstream fiction, is limited in the novel to resisted temptation. In another apparently sanitized account of the meeting written 11 years after the fact, he calls her Mlle Pauline and describes her at the masquerade as being 'about five-and-thirty years of age' in a 'disgusting old dress', a costume in 'the fashion of the time of Louis XV'. And though he claims to have visited her chambers, where 'I believe the woman did her duty perfectly well in her station', for the purpose of picking up some shirts she made for him, he reveals enough of her life history to suggest he had spent considerably more time with her than a chance encounter at a party or a brief visit of business.[36]

At the examinations that year Thackeray ended in the second class, dashing any hopes for an honours degree. Thackeray left Cambridge for good in June, having accumulated about £1500 in gambling debts. There is no evidence to suggest that his parents were aware of that fact. Many is the lad in his fiction who runs up debts with promises to pay when an inheritance comes due and whose accounts of bills, in letters home, fail to tell the whole story.

Thackeray's bid for independence, however, still entailed getting permission from his mother, for he was yet two years from majority and from his inheritance. He argued for his next venture, an extended stay in Germany, on the grounds that he would learn the language, read deeply and get to know societies other than his own. Somehow, his view prevailed. Intending to join the English society of Dresden, he stopped instead at Weimar for six months, from where he requested and obtained, through the help of Major Carmichael-Smyth, a cornetcy in the Devon yeomanry and the uniform that went with it, which was his real object, since everyone in the Weimar society seemed to be an officer of something. His letters home contain humorous accounts of falling in love with two

*Figure 3.3* Pegasus in harness with cart. Drawing in Thackeray's copy of the poems of Schiller. Reproduced with permission from the Harry Ransom Humanities Center and Mrs Norman Butler representing the estate of W.M. Thackeray

young ladies who abandoned him for better prospects, of meeting Wolfgang von Goethe and the intellectual circle presided over by his daughter-in-law Ottilie von Goethe, of studying German and things in general with Dr Friedrich August Wilhelm Weissenborn and of reading and translating Schiller's poetry. He wrote poetry, a play and essays, or at least started them; but he published nothing while in Germany. And in his copy of Schiller's poems he had already doodled the figure of Pegasus in harness drawing a carriage, an image he returned to repeatedly as indicative of his own relationship to high art.[37] Even more now than at college Thackeray was free to follow his own bent, and he seems to have cut a relatively graceful figure in the little Prussian capital. Though he claimed German philosophy was too heavy for him, he took readily to the worldly wisdom, skepticism, tolerance and suspended judgment of Weimar's rather relaxed society.[38] The importance of his newly acquired uniform suggested he was still a somewhat self-centered would-be English rake. Unlike George Osborne, however, his sense of humor under cut any pretentiousness in his self-indulgence. In a letter home he admits to being still passionately in love, only with a different girl, and lamenting that he didn't know what he would do in two weeks' time when he expected once again to be free. Furthermore, he was also showing the tendencies of mind that led him to Victor Cousin's popular philosophy of uncertainty, which he read in 1832,[39] and Montaigne's amused, cynical, detached observations of life in the *Essays*, which Thackeray read and reread throughout his life.

Returning to England just before his twentieth birthday in July 1831, Thackeray spent a few weeks at Larkbeare where with his mother and stepfather he surveyed the options before him. Though he would not absolutely have to work for a living, he had to do something. His own inclinations led him away from the Church and the Army, and parental pressure to be conventionally respectable kept him, at least for the moment, from painting and writing. He compromised on the law. But the choice proved temporary. His reading, clerking and dining to order in the Middle Temple could not survive the joking and disparaging attitudes revealed in his letters home and to Edward Fitzgerald, who occasionally came up to London to roam the streets and go to plays with him. That year, also, his friendship with Harry Kemble, the black sheep son of the famous acting family (Charles Kemble was his father; Fanny Kemble was his sister), provided more dissipation, gambling and raucous nights – resulting in repeated entries in his diary vowing reform. His friendship with the editor of *Fraser's Magazine*, William Maginn, beginning in the Spring of 1832, was both exhilarating and disappointing. Though it would be two years before Thackeray's writings began appearing in *Fraser's*, his introduction to Maginn's world seems to have begun when, by Thackeray's account, Maginn took him to a 'common brothel where I left him, very much disgusted & sickened,' but it is not clear that he would always react in that way.[40] Surprisingly, his law studies lasted nearly a year, during which his passion for the theatre and reading fiction and history steadily edged out the law. In June, a month before his inheritance came to him, he abandoned his seat in the Temple, and, for a lark, electioneered on behalf of his friend, Charles Buller, campaigning successfully for a seat from Cornwall in the newly reformed Parliament. Thackeray undertook the task in spite of his allegiance to the Tories and Wellington, against whom Buller stood.

Coming of age on 18 July 1832, Thackeray's first business was to pay old gambling debts, an act which did not cure his craving for cards and dice. With a remaining fortune between £15 000 and £17 000, there was no reason for Thackeray to apply himself seriously to any profession that did not completely appeal to him. Back in London, but still without a viable avocation or vocation and without an entrée to the circles of society which his fortune and his public school education had led him to expect, he undertook a variety of 'ungentlemanly' pursuits, including bill discounting (purchasing post-dated IOUs at a reduced rate and holding them to maturity for the full value) and desultory journalism.

More significantly, however, he turned his attention seriously to art. Thackeray next spent several months in Paris, enjoying the independence of his inheritance, casting about pleasurably but without purpose, and recording feelings of guilt and unhappiness in his diary. It was in these months that Thackeray came closest to being the young cad, the British ideal of a self-centered dandy exemplified by George Osborne in *Vanity Fair.* Lazy, dissipated, unable to commit himself to any purpose, he noted in his diary, 'I must mend, or else I shall be poor idle and wicked most likely in a couple more years.'[41] An obvious discomfort with that life eventually brought him back to become a writer who understood both the details and the attractions of the lifestyle.

Then, in a bid to do something serious with his life, he purchased the journal *The National Standard* in early 1833, and with James Hume as subeditor, he acted as editor and provided the bulk of copy. In 10 months the venture ended in failure, but Thackeray during that time joined the Garrick Club and the London literary circles to which he would return after yet another venture into France to take up his next 'real' profession, painting.

But financial disaster struck as a sort of mixed blessing, changing the course of Thackeray's life. His gambling had cost him perhaps a fifth of his fortune in his first year, but by December 1833, a series of bank failures in India reduced Thackeray's inheritance by over £11 000, leaving perhaps as much as £7000, the income of which was, however, entirely committed in annuities to his half sister and his mother. Thackeray may have had as much a £100 a year for himself, but now there was every reason for him to make good on the resolves that had peppered his diary for over two years.

At first, it appeared that *The National Standard* might give him a competence, but painting was a fond aspiration still, and he dabbled

*Figure 3.4* George Osborne lighting a cigar with a letter from Amelia, *Vanity Fair*, 135

in the art studios while writing as Paris Correspondent for the paper. Both his literary and artistic careers were originally undertaken as fulfillments of pleasure by a man of modest independent fortune filling his days. The work turned serious when the independence was lost, but the lessons of life that would change him from the George Osborne-like character into the mature Thackeray were just beginning.

*The National Standard* failing in early 1834, Thackeray embarked on what was supposed to be a three-year painter's apprenticeship in the ateliers of a French artist. There is evident relief in the diary entries expressing thanks to God for making him poor, thereby enabling resolve to triumph over lassitude. It would take more than poverty, however, to reform this young dandy. Thackeray's initial devotion to the new profession ended within a year, when he determined that his talent for comic drawings would never develop into the skills and styles required by the tastes of his day in serious art. Failure to succeed in a profession from which family and friends had sought to dissuade him in the first place was a bitter pill to swallow. The feeling is captured exactly in *The Newcomes* when Major Pendennis, upon hearing that Clive Newcome was to be a painter, objected that the 'calling' was on a par with hairdressing and cooking, not work for a gentleman. By summer, 1835, virtually penniless, disgusted with his inadequate talent, with the vulgarity of his artist friends, with the moral degradation of his gambling cronies, one of whom committed suicide that spring, and with his own repeated failures to reform or succeed, Thackeray's bohemian sojourn reached a nadir of depression.

It seems almost a cliché to say that Thackeray then met a girl unlike any he had known hitherto, fell in love, and began to turn his life around. Isabella Shawe was a shy diminutive, not especially pretty girl, indulged and almost wholly dominated by her widowed mother. The father, a distinguished colonel in India and southeast Asia, died after 12 years of marriage leaving Mrs Shawe with five children living on a pension and what small investments the Colonel had made. To make ends meet, they moved to Paris where, in the company of similar English families of modest means, appearances could be maintained. Had Thackeray's circle of acquaintance included only the painters and dissipated young men, his preferred companions, he might never have met Isabella. But his relatives the Ritchies and the family of Eyre Evans Crowe provided him frequent society of a more genteel sort. Even so, it was unlikely that any mother would encourage such as suitor as Thackeray who, having moved from his increasingly cantankerous grandmother Butler's apartment to a dingy but peaceful den, was without a profession and whose great expectations lay in the past.

Falling in love, however, focused Thackeray's ambitions, providing a drive hitherto lacking. Determined to 'win and wear' Isabella as his wife, Thackeray wrote for both *Galignani's Messenger* and a rival English paper and perhaps did hack editorial work for them as well. And with the backing of *Galignani's* owner, John Bowes Bowes,

Thackeray published his first book *Flore et Zéphyr*, a collection of captioned lithographs, which gained neither attention nor money. The book shows both Thackeray's fascination with and criticism of opera and his bent for satire. Both Bowes and Thackeray blamed the publisher, John Mitchell, in London, whom they suspected did better on the publication than either the artist/author or his financial backer. Then, perhaps something about Thackeray's new outlook encouraged his step-father, Colonel Carmichael-Smyth, to join with some other members of the waning Radical Party to become a major underwriter for a journal of radical politics, *The Constitutional and Public Ledger*.

As Paris Correspondent for *The Constitutional*, with an income of eight guineas a week, Thackeray proposed to Isabella in April 1836, much to the chagrin of her mother who decided she had allowed that little friendship entirely too much leeway. In a mild replay of Thackeray's maternal grandmother's protective action on behalf of Anne Becher, Mrs Shawe confined Isabella and banned Thackeray. But the girl fell ill, the mother panicked, the young man succeeded in communicating by means of a loyal (or disloyal) servant, and Isabella found the courage to challenge her mother's authority and the validity of her objections to her lover. Courtship was resumed and the couple married on 20 August. The conflict with the mother-in-law was, however, just the beginning of a long battle. Mrs Shawe became the prototype for many an impossible mother-in-law in Thackeray's fiction.

The marriage was, at first, a very happy one, though beset by problems. He took his bride to London and began 10 years of heavy hack work, living from hand to mouth and suffering from one domestic and financial disaster after another. *The Constitutional* failed in July 1837, one month after the birth of Thackeray's first daughter, Anne Isabella (later Lady Ritchie, a future novelist in her own right). The demise of the paper left Thackeray and his small family without support except what could be gained by freelance writing. Two more daughters were born, Jane (who died at 8 months) in 1838, and Harriet Marian ('Minnie,' later Mrs Leslie Stephen) in 1840. Jane's death and Minnie's birth brought on serious depression in Isabella compounded by feelings of worthlessness as mother, wife and housekeeper and by neglect from Thackeray who, finding he could get no work done at home, spent more and more time away, researching his travel narratives and writing essays and stories, primarily for *Fraser's Magazine*.

In the first years the happy young husband, father and budding writer turned very industrious. From the demise of *The Constitutional* in July 1837 to the end of 1840, Thackeray published 90 magazine pieces, including most notably the work that became known as *The Yellowplush Papers*. Written from the point of view of a footman with comically bad orthography but satirically sharp social insight, this series grew from a stand-alone essay to a series held together primarily by the narrator's persona. It incorporated Thackeray's first extended fictional account of the doings of Algernon Percy Deuceace, a gambling, womanizing, fortune-hunting scoundrel based at least in part on Henry Matthews, the college friend and 'rook' (card shark) to whom Thackeray had played 'pigeon' (victim). Before this series was quite completed it had been reprinted in book form in Philadelphia. If one were to call *Flore et Zéphyr* a book, one could call *Yellowplush* Thackeray's second book, except that he did not hear about its publication till much later, for it was 'pirated' and not paid for – a perfectly legal theft by the American publisher, since there was no international copyright law to protect the author's interests.

The most substantial single magazine essay in these early years was his critical assessment of the artist George Cruikshank for the *Westminster Review* in June 1840. Thackeray's friend and neighbor, William Cole, had arranged for the work and magazine publication and paid for it, but when the work turned out as well as it did, Cole decided to reissue it in book form. Negotiations for revision and for additional payment both fell victim to missed communications, so that in the end, though *An Essay on the Genius of George Cruikshank* was issued as a paperbound pamphlet, Thackeray's third book, there was no additional income for the author.

Thackeray's fourth book was his first 'real' book, the first for which he was paid. *The Paris Sketch Book*, combined new material with a number of his first magazine publications. Thackeray had offered the as yet unwritten book to the publisher in January of 1837; it was finished in June of 1840. Its modest success and the author's continuing financial need spurred him to enter a curious contract with a new publisher for a similar book on Ireland. This time he managed to get an advance, but he had to have his stepfather and his cousin sign an agreement to repay the advance if Thackeray failed to produce the book, and the publisher, Chapman and Hall, kept the writer's chest of plateware (silver or plated utensils and dinner ware) as additional surety. The date was September 1840; the contract was for two volumes by 31 December! Even in good times, it could hardly be reasonable to suspect such a deadline could be met, and these were not good times. The book was not finished until 1843, and the publisher held the plate chest until 1846.

Perhaps frantic activity kept Thackeray from noticing the seriousness of his shy wife's mental condition, but in mid-August 1840, returning from a two-week trip in Holland and Belgium where he gathered materials for a guide book never finished, he was alarmed by the 'languor and depression' in his wife. It happened that his mother-in-law had by this time moved from Paris to Cork, and Thackeray's desire to seek help for Isabella turned his attention to Ireland. Need and anxiety probably drove him as much as authorial pride to the contract for the *Irish Sketch-Book*. On 13 September, the small family embarked for Ireland.

In September 1840, hoping that the company of her mother and favorite sister Jane would help restore her spirits, Thackeray took the ailing Isabella to Ireland. In the crossing, Isabella threw herself from a water closet into the sea from which she was eventually rescued, but it was no longer possible to avoid knowledge of her mental breakdown. The Irish sojourn, originally planned as a research trip for *The Irish Sketch-Book* turned into a domestic battle with the mother-in-law, from which Thackeray and Isabella fled after four weeks. In debt to his grandmother and indebted in incalculable ways to his children's nurse, Brodie, and with an advance from the publishers Chapman and Hall for an Irish book which he had been unable to research or write, Thackeray returned to his parents in Paris, where he managed, over the next six months to write 10 magazine pieces, a small book (*The Second Funeral of Napoleon*), a serial novelette (*The History of Samuel Titmarsh*) and several chapters of a novel never finished (*The Knights of Borsellen*). From November 1840 to February 1842, Isabella was in and out of professional care, her condition waxing and waning, but in the long run deteriorating until she was placed with Dr Puzin at Chaillot, where she lapsed into a stable, detached condition of unawareness of the world around her. In October 1845 she was taken to England and placed with a home nurse, where she survived placidly for 30 years after Thackeray himself had died.

No one thing could have changed Thackeray as profoundly as he seems to have changed in the last months of that awful year of 1840. The responsibilities of a family had made him not so much a workaholic as a binge worker, seeking and accepting every deadline possible and focusing on each task until it was done, with little regard for the rest of the world. And when each writing task was finished, he sought out sources of stimulation for additional writing: coffee-house talk, clubs and travel. His wife's illness caught his attention, as nothing else ever had. His sense of guilt appears finally to have produced more than repeated self-recriminations in a diary. His attention to Isabella and his daughters and his acceptance of his part in creating their condition and his responsibility for their future raised his consciousness about their restraints and vulnerabilities, their worth and potential. In the next few months he would learn to feel keenly the willing sacrifice made on his behalf by Brodie, the servant who postponed her wedding to accompany the ailing family to Ireland in search of relief. From his works, particularly from *The History of Samuel Titmarsh and the Great Hoggarty Diamond* (serialized from September 1841) and *A Shabby Genteel Story*, begun before the crisis but written largely after, it is clear that Thackeray began thinking self-consciously about the self-important self-centeredness of his own life as well as that of ordinary men, his peers, whose birthright was to enjoy life and use wives and other women-folk as superior servants. His narratives of young men pursuing normal courses of self-fulfillment depict more and more accurately the women who suffered and supported them.

It is not so much that Thackeray wrote his own narrative into the stories of Sam Titmarsh and, later, Arthur Pendennis, though to be sure he did that; rather, it is that there is a feminine light cast on the treatment of ordinary young Englishmen with ordinary notions of ambition, expectations, manly pleasures, and the adoration of their handsome beings and doings by doting women taking the form of mothers, wives and other servants. Thackeray's fiction manages to put the women's view forward even when the male characters fail to see it. The author and the reader, together, assess the unhappy results of ordinary men behaving ordinarily. A criticism of what passes for normal is the result. I believe it was the sensitizing effect of the five years from the autumn of 1840 to October 1845, during which Thackeray tried to tend personally to his wife's illness, taking her from one doctor to another and to health spas, that burned into his heart and mind 'how such admirable creatures tend and suffer with one'[42] and the necessity 'to be interested in their ways & amusements, to be cheerful & constant at home: frugal & orderly if possible'.[43]

Inevitably, Thackeray's increased awareness of the real conditions of women and children was accompanied by a parallel awareness of male insensitivity. And the fact that his new view might be temporary – maintained only during the time of hurt – is evident not so much from any backsliding in Thackeray's own life as from the point of view maintained by Arthur Pendennis. Thackeray's portrayal of Pendennis, 'hero' of his second major work and narrator of most of the later works, constitutes a major study of masculine self-absorption in a man of intelligence who has the ability to learn and to see beyond the blinkered line of sight of which most men are capable but who is slow to learn and internalize his own insights. Pendennis learned and relearned and then forgot to understand the cruelties to women that passed as ordinary behaviour for sons, lovers, husbands and fathers. It is apparent that Thackeray's criticism of men in Victorian society did not stop with exposing the gross cruelties of men who took women for granted in a land where marriage laws deprived women of any legal standing whatsoever; Thackeray developed in Pendennis a continuing study of kind cruelty and benign insensitivity, as will be discussed later.

Among Thackeray's early exposures of such men is Sam Titmarsh whose fortunes flare and funk, leaving him chastened and dependent upon his resourceful, strong and loving wife, whose economic contribution to the family, in the end, equals her husband's. Mary Titmarsh may be based in part on Isabella – having her deference and subservient mien – but unlike the novelist's wife, Mary proves resilient and sensible, capable of rescuing a husband from the consequences of his own ignorance and impetuous self-confidence.

The experiences of these years left other effects, not all of them scars. Thackeray's humor became more complex. It was no less clear-sighted than before, but the admixture of compassion and of self-mockery already present in his early satiric writings becomes more obviously self-deprecating, admitting the author's complicity in the failings being exposed for laughter. Like his great 18th-century master, Henry Fielding, he grew to reject satire and the burlesque, as cruel and silly. Instead he found the normal exercise of human vanity and hypocrisy – the exaggeration of small virtues and the pretense to absent virtues – sufficiently ridiculous for comic purposes. There is a bitter-sweetness to Thackeray's sometimes sad laughter that is taken for sentimentality by readers who prefer hard-hitting Swiftean sarcasm. But as will be argued later, satire had become not only alien to Thackeray's personal experience of life, it was philosophically opposed to his rather unusual understanding of human experience. Satire requires a sense of rightness or even righteousness which Thackeray understood to be personal not universal. His words of wisdom tend to echo Jesus' words to the righteous crowd bent on punishing a sinner, 'Let him that is without sin among you cast the first stone,' rather than the cry of the multitude in Pontius Pilate's courtyard, 'Crucify him, crucify him.'

The experience of his mother-in-law's cruelties in contrast to the support of Brodie, his own mother and of his cousin and virtual sister, Mary Graham Carmichael, created in Thackeray deep understandings of women's capacities for cruelty, demands, devotion and generosity that can be seen in his complex portraits of women such as Amelia Sedley and Helen Pendennis who exact dreadful tolls from the men they control through helpless love, and of women like Blanche Amory, Becky Sharp and Beatrix Esmond who exercise control through imperious sexuality, and like Ethel Newcome and Laura Pendennis whose native intelligence and humor are the objects of male repression and societal control. All of these women have secret depths, intelligence and emotional complexities that Thackeray reveals in ways that some readers have taken to be inconsistency of characterization.

# 4
# Professional Writer and Literary Lion

In the six years from the manifestation of Isabella's insanity at the end of 1840 to the commencement of the serial publication of *Vanity Fair* in January 1847, Thackeray published 386 magazine pieces and three books, all under pseudonyms. There are 53 known pseudonyms, the most famous and clearly differentiated narrative personas being George Savage Fitzboodle, Michael Angelo Titmarsh, Major Gahagan (the Irish braggadocio soldier whose memoirs of Indian and Spanish wars make up *The Tremendous Adventures of Major Gahagan*), Ikey Solomons (named for a criminal family and the author of satirical 'Newgate' sensational stories such as *Catherine*) and Charles James Yellowplush (the quintessential literary footman whose fractured vocabulary never cracks the dignified façade of a perfect snob).

It is debatable if Thackeray's use of pseudonyms reflected a desire for anonymity as a writer, but he developed through the device a remarkable range of ventriloquist voices and a habit of presentation which dominated the later works, written in the persona of Arthur Pendennis, an admitted alter ego who nevertheless undergoes remarkable analysis and complex criticism by the 'author' whose defenses of Pendennis are full of apparently deliberate holes. The result is either a clumsy and inept narrative technique that allows readers, used to taking Victorian authors at face value, to equate Pendennis with Thackeray and to conclude, therefore, that Pen's false starts and contradictions represent Thackeray's lack of control over his medium; or the narrative device is a subtle and complex technique in which the ordinary and conventional but above-average intellect, language and behavior of the narrator do not prevent his exposure – at least not to those who distinguish author from narrator – for his inconsistency of character, insensitivity and lack of self-awareness. The effect, to those who hold this latter position, which is more charitable to the author than to the narrator, is a sense of ever-increasing narrative complexity and subtlety, a finer and sharper criticism of social conventions. To less sympathetic readers, Thackeray's later fiction represents exhaustion, a loss of control and vision, for such readers do not credit him with vision above and beyond that of his narrator.

Having placed his wife in the care of Dr Puzin in 1842, Thackeray returned to London, leaving his daughters for the next four years with his mother in Paris. London was where he could earn by writing what was needed to support his family and make his way in the world. At first he lived in the family house at 13 Great Coram Street, which he shared uneasily with his cousin Mary Graham and her new husband Charles Carmichael (brother of Major Henry Carmichael-Smyth). Thackeray's first contribution to *Punch* appeared, but almost immediately he undertook the long deferred research trip to Ireland, spending five months there. Though he had reviewed the Irish novelist Charles Lever rather roughly, their meeting was cordial and their bumpy friendship lasted for life. Thackeray dedicated *The Irish Sketch-Book* to Lever, who reviewed it admiringly in the *Dublin Review*, though he obviously had reservations about Thackeray's Cockney portrait of Ireland. The friendship was not helped much by Thackeray's parody of Lever's work in the series of *Punch's Prize Novelists* four years later, and Lever returned the favor by caricaturing Thackeray as Elias Howle in *Roland Cashel*. But in the 1860s, when hard times came to Lever, he turned to Thackeray for advice on London publishers. Returning to London, Thackeray gave up the house, moving first to a hotel and then to fourth-floor lodgings in Jermyn St, where he tried to take up his old bachelor life. Judging from his letters, however, he never after lost consciousness of two daughters he longed to have with him again.

He next undertook travel in Belgium to revive the travel book project he had abandoned the year before, when he had returned to find his wife in a deep depression; but again this traveler's guide to the Low Countries failed to emerge. During this time Thackeray lived the life of an ineligible bachelor, frequently invited to dinners, but always on the verge of loneliness, and he revived the theatre-going, club-haunting, late-night life of the days before marriage. The only real difference was that now he was writing for his life, seriously committed to the grind of 'odious magazinery', driven by want, and by the ambition to leave his daughters the same inheritance he had briefly had and then lost.

He had written a short novel, *Catherine*, in 1838, published a collection of *Comic Tales*, in 1840, and another serial novelette, *The History of Samuel Titmarsh*, in 1841. He began to think seriously of a full-length novel, though it would have to be serialized, since he could not afford the time to complete it before receiving remuneration, and he had not yet convinced publishers to provide significant advances. Though the *Irish Sketch-Book* appeared in 1843, Chapman and Hall, his publishers, still held the author's chest of plate – perhaps because Thackeray had no use for it in a fourth-floor walk-up lodging.

What most readers consider Thackeray's first real novel, *Barry Lyndon*, began its serial course in January 1844 in *Fraser's Magazine*. It was, however, more of a potential novel always in danger of being discontinued, than it was a triumphal entry. Written in the style of Fielding's *Jonathan Wild*, it does represent a major advance over his early fiction in characterization, narrative technique, plot construction and complexity of themes, but readers of *Fraser's Magazine* were apparently unprepared to distinguish easily between a ruffian's bragging autobiographical voice and that of a satirical author exposing both the egoisms of the character and the chicanery of the society in which he bilked and was bilked. Thackeray was, in addition, poking a stick in the eye of readers who enjoyed sentimentalized stories of victim criminals, such as those made famous by William Harrison Ainsworth and Edward Bulwer Lytton, both of whom made tidy sums from fictional autobiographies of fictional criminals. Barry Lyndon asked readers to agree with him in his criminal pursuit of the main chance and his egomaniacal care for his own over anyone else's needs. Readers' dislike for the character of Barry Lyndon extended to the author, and so the magazine's editors asked him to shut the story down after 10 installments. *Barry Lyndon* remains, however, a critically acclaimed and highly regarded first novel.

Thackeray, in any case, was willing to bring *Barry Lyndon* to a halt because in August, on three days' notice, he undertook a three-month trip to the Mediterranean with stops in Spain, Greece,

Turkey, the Holy Land and Egypt, recounted in frequent *Punch* essays signed 'From Our Fat Contributor' and, more meditatively, in *Notes of a Journey from Cornhill to Grand Cairo* (1846). Comical recollections survive, in his letters home, of Thackeray's severe difficulties in writing three works at once – *Barry Lyndon, Fat Contributor* and *Cornhill to Cairo* – cudgeling his brains while fighting Mediterranean heat by day, ship-board bedbugs by night and seasickness at every storm. The Cockney's view of the world, which was a chief element in his Paris and Irish travel books, dominates the writing of the eastern stories; for Thackeray acknowledged to himself that visitors bring as much of their view of the world with them as they find on their travels, and he eschewed pontificating. The flavor of this point of view is caught by the three cheers for *Punch* allegedly led by Thackeray from the top of an Egyptian pyramid. The trip took just three months, though on returning to Italy all who disembarked at Malta were quarantined for 15 days. Finally reaching Rome, Thackeray expected mail and money from his publisher/bankers, Chapman and Hall, but instead, as he recounted in a letter to them on 10 January:

> I looked 35 days running at the Post Office until I was sick and ashamed of applying[. T]he beasts would not give me your letters because they were supposed to be for Mr. Jackeray instead of Thackeray.... the money was quite safe at Tortoni's, where the clerks had declined to have anything to do with my bills, and where as soon as they found them covered they invited me to a ball.... For the last 3 weeks my annoyance has been so great at receiving no letters that I've done nothing.... I cant pardon them the bitterness of my feelings as I turned away day after day from the dd dd-dd-ddd-ddd post office.[44]

Back in London in April 1845, Thackeray moved to slightly better bachelor quarters in St James's Street where in June he was visited by his mother and children, who still lived in Paris. And in October he had his hopelessly ill Isabella moved from the sanitarium in France and installed in Camberwell with a Mrs Bakewell in whose care she remained the rest of her life. One more move, in June 1846, to Young St, put Thackeray in a house to which he invited his parents and to which he brought his daughters in September. His parents, however, chose to stay in Paris out of the reach of the Major's London creditors. Though Thackeray paid the Major's debts off with income from *Vanity Fair* and *Pendennis* in 1848, thus clearing the way for the paternal couple's return to England, they chose to remain in Paris until 1859.

Although Thackeray continued to contribute heavily to *Fraser's Magazine,* and was a regular contributor to the *Foreign Quarterly Review* and the *Morning Chronicle,* in the 1840s *Punch* was increasingly his primary periodical affiliation, and the magazine's weekly staff dinners became an important social and intellectual function in his life until his resignation in December 1851.

In 1846 *Punch* began publishing Thackeray's comprehensive and exhaustive analysis of 'The Snobs of England. By One of Themselves' (March 1846 to February 1847), and in the next year he wrote a series of parodies of novelists G.P.R. James, Charles Lever, Mrs Gore, Edward Bulwer, Benjamin Disraeli and James Fenimore Cooper, in 'Punch's Prize Novelists' (April to October 1847). These serials gained him genuine, first-class popular standing and prepared the way thematically for *Vanity Fair.* It is, furthermore, not unimportant that it was the publishers of *Punch,* Bradbury and Evans, who published Thackeray's four great serial novels: *Vanity Fair* (1847–48), *Pendennis* (1848–50), *The Newcomes* (1853–55) and *The Virginians* (1857–59).

By the late 1840s, Thackeray was increasingly seen as the chief writer in stature and popularity for *Punch,* though Douglas Jerrold, author of many popular plays and of one of the magazine's most popular series, *Mrs Caudle's Curtain Lectures,* was the more prolific contributor and felt he had a greater commitment to the magazine. Furthermore, Jerrold and Thackeray as chief *Punch* rivals did not mesh well, for they were from different sides of the track socially and clashed in manners, religion and politics. Thackeray was a free thinker by this time, but his reverence for the sacred was never lost. Jerrold, on the other hand, was openly scornful and particularly nasty about the Catholics. It did not help the 'friendship' that Richard Doyle, one of the magazine's best illustrators, was Catholic and a good friend of Thackeray's. The last straw, in Thackeray's view, came when *Punch* published a particularly cutting political caricature of Louis Napoleon, otherwise known as Napoleon III, Emperor of France, whom Thackeray had championed. There is conflicting evidence about just who said what to whom, but the upshot was that Thackeray resigned. It happened, however, that Thackeray was under contract to another publisher, George Smith, for the calendar year of 1852, during which he was not allowed to publish anything anywhere. And he did publish nine times in *Punch* in 1853, when the Smith injunction was lifted. The resignation in 1851, therefore, may have been a mere gesture.

Nothing he had written thus far, however, quite prepared readers for the panoramic scope, the protean voice, or the seriousness and complexity of comic vision incorporated in *Vanity Fair*, begun in January 1847 and running for 19 months as the first publication to bear the name William Makepeace Thackeray on the title page. Though the print run and sales for the novel's initial serial part were under 5000 copies and though Thackeray complained that its popularity did not match its critical success, 1847 proved a watershed year, separating Thackeray's struggling hackwork from the success that brought publishers begging to his door. He made £1200 plus a share of profits from *Vanity Fair*, and each novel thereafter earned him more than the previous one till the last years of his life when his income exceeded £7000 a year. His primary publishers in the 1840s had been Chapman and Hall, who besides the Irish and Mediterranean travel books published four Christmas volumes. It was rumored that *Vanity Fair* was turned down by five or more publishers before Bradbury and Evans, the proprietors of *Punch*, agreed to publish it in the same format and style they used for their star author, Charles Dickens.

But a third publisher, George Smith, eventually became the major force in Thackeray's writing career. In Smith's first approach, he offered Thackeray £1000 for his next book, sight unseen, but Thackeray was already committed and counter-offered a Christmas book, *The Kickleburys on the Rhine* (dated 1851 but published in December 1850). In June 1851, Smith signed the novelist to a £1200 contract for a novel in three volumes, stipulating that he could publish nothing else in the six months before or after publication – which turned out to be the calendar year of 1852. Smith, known as the prince of publishers, was generous with his money and ruthless in his control; for Thackeray had averaged 59 magazine publications a year from 1847 through 1851 in addition to two major serials. In 1852 he had but one publication, *Henry Esmond*, in three volumes.

But Smith's contract said nothing about not delivering lectures, and Thackeray had already planned a series on 18th-century English humourists, which he began delivering in London and other major cities in England and Scotland, making more money, more friends, and more future readers from lectures in 1852 than from his published writings in any previous year.[45] Upon publication of *Esmond* in October 1852, he took his lecture tour to America for five months, visiting New York, Boston, Providence, Philadelphia, Baltimore, Washington (where he dined with out-going President Fillmore and in-coming President Pierce and lobbied, unsuccessfully, with both on behalf of international copyright), Richmond, Charleston and Savannah. The lectures were published in England as soon as the contractual time of silence expired and just as Thackeray returned from America. On a second tour of America from October 1855 to April 1856, he lectured on the Four Georges – the four Hanoverian Kings named George who occupied England's throne from 1714 to 1830. This time he added upstate New York to the itinerary in the north and Alabama, Louisiana, Missouri and Ohio in the south and west. Thackeray's income from the second lecture tour was accumulating, and he invested in American railways and in the trans-Atlantic cable. Needless to say, the Civil War, five years later, wiped out most of his American railroad investment and cost overruns damaged his cable shares.

Thackeray's encounters with American publishers, who had appropriated and republished his early work at will, was remarkably different from those by Charles Dickens and Anthony Trollope who both lost their tempers over their lack of control of American publications. Thackeray, acknowledging that half a loaf was better than no loaf, laughed and befriended the American publishers: James Fields in Boston, George Putnam in Philadelphia, and, in New York the Appletons and the Harper Brothers, who were the biggest pirates of them all. He negotiated courtesy contracts, since no law existed to require any contracts at all. The Harper Brothers had pirated both *Vanity Fair* and *Pendennis* with no compensation to the author, who in a friendly way, upon meeting James Harper's young daughter, remarked, 'So this is a "pirate's" daughter, is it?'.[46] But his basic attitude is captured in a letter to a Philadelphia publisher, George P. Putnam, declining a generous bid to publish Thackeray's current lectures because he felt a loyalty to his new friends at Harpers whose earlier bid he had already accepted: 'All things considered, I think it best that I should accept their liberal proposal. I thank you very much for your generous offer; and for my own sake, as well as that of my literary brethren in England, I am sincerely rejoiced to find how very kindly the American publishers are disposed towards us.'[47] Even in his letters home Thackeray acknowledges that the person-to-person relations he was establishing with American publishers was leading to financial relations that alone would have made the trip worthwhile.

Thackeray's home had been at Young St for nine years, but he was often away. Returning from New York at the end of April 1853, he was off again to the Continent by early July for a tour of Germany and Switzerland with his daughters, during which trip he began writing *The Newcomes*. Spending September and October in London to launch that novel, he took his daughters to Italy for the winter, returning in April only to move from Young St to Onslow Square, Brompton. One month after moving, he was again on the Continent for two and half months. Thackeray is famous as a novelist for his observation of things, of the stuff of life, particularly of the fribbles and vanities to which people attach themselves or even use to measure their own worth. But his connection with or attachment to his own things and his house seems to have been either casual or so confident that he did not make much fuss of them. Although he was in London for the move from Young St to Onslow Sq., he spent a few nights in a hotel 'till Brompton's ready: poor old Kensington became intolerably melumcholy [sic] and I'm glad as usual to get away from it without a parting'.[48] He left others to take care of the move, and though avoiding partings was Thackeray's characteristic way of avoiding a sentimental scene, his schedule shows how frequently he seems to have been 'glad to get away' from his house.

Writing *The Newcomes* was not a smooth or simple operation. Thackeray had written two major serials before and had a lifetime of magazine deadlines in his experience. Furthermore, he was at first determined to avoid, if at all possible, the desperate anxiety and pressure that had usually attended the hand to mouth feeding of the insatiable printing machine, which was the case when he wrote his installments in the month they were to be published. So, with this novel, he intended to write it first, or a substantial portion, and avoid the stress of monthly deadlines. By 1 October, when the first number was published, he was writing number five and feeling comfortable enough to arrange for an editor, Percival Leigh from the *Punch* staff, to oversee the monthly production, while he and his daughters spent the winter in Rome. But, of course, things would go wrong. Number five turned out to be three pages too long; three pages of number six mailed from Rome seem never to have arrived; proofs which could have been sent to Thackeray months in advance arrived in the old style, just before they were needed. One result is that major revisions in number six seem to have been undertaken by Leigh, who rescued the discarded pages from chapter five to make up for the three pages missing from chapter six and seems to have taken the opportunity to tweak many of the sentences. But in the end, *The Newcomes* was declared by the reviewers to be Thackeray's best so far. He himself is reported to have said 'I can't jump farther than I did in *The Newcomes*.'[49] Indeed, many 20th-century critics have praised it for its rich, detailed, 'thick' descriptive and evocative qualities.[50]

Thackeray felt the trips to the Continent were necessary to remind him of the scenes of this youth, which Clive Newcome would revisit in the novel; for, as with *Pendennis*, many of the author's own experiences were written into the new tale. The failure of Bundlecund Bank that ruined Colonel Newcome is reminiscent of the bank failure that ruined Thackeray and from which he was in part recovering by writing *The Newcomes*. Ethel Newcome seems to derive in part from Sally Baxter whose bold honesty and irony is revealed in scenes like the one in the art gallery where she wears a 'sold' tag from a painting, indicating her status in the marriage market. Ethel may also derive in part from Mrs Brookfield whose attractions Thackeray never actually outgrew. It is even probable that Blanch Stanley, a woman admired forlornly by Richard Doyle, Thackeray's friend and illustrator of *The Newcomes*, can be traced in Ethel's character. Clive Newcome may derive in part from the artist Doyle, but he obviously is also drawn from Thackeray's own youthful longing but failed attempt to be a painter. Colonel Newcome is modeled in part on Thackeray's stepfather, Major Carmichael-Smyth, whom he both admired and condescended to. But the Colonel is also modeled on Sir Charles Grandison and Don Quixote, whose adventures Thackeray re-read in September 1853.[51]

Thackeray had pointed out in *Vanity Fair* that it took three generations to make a gentleman. Certainly the story of Osborne, Sr, the wealthy tradesman who lived in the City, and George, his son, who was sent away to school and who consorted with the sons and daughters of the West End, and who bitterly disappointed his father by marrying Amelia, also from the City, instead of attaching the family to the aristocracy, and finally Georgie, who was taken from his mother to be raised genteelly – that story illustrates the principle of its taking three generations to make a gentleman – or in this case an apparent gentleman. *The Newcomes* by its title and the name of its central family is another illustration of the attempt. The Newcome family, occasionally actually referred to as 'Newcomers', is obviously on the make in the three areas that matter most: money, blood and religion. It would be at least 10 more years before Matthew Arnold, in *Culture and Anarchy*, would define the class of English newcomers whose two great fears were poverty and Hell and whose conspicuous consumption and toadying to the nobility would be labeled 'philistine'. But Thackeray has portrayed the class in detail, demonstrating that great shows of religious virtue do not prevent calculated business ventures or manipulative marital campaigns to ally the newcoming family with old blood; its India merchants and soldiers coming back to England with small fortunes; its bankers using and abusing their customers, including their own family; its mothers pursuing advantageous marriage partners for their daughters. In short, it is the tale of a most respectable family – a large one with characters as diverse as the supposedly gentle and good-hearted Colonel Newcome, who famously died answering 'Adsum' to his name in the roll call of Heaven, and the scoundrel and rascal, his nephew, Barnes, whose discarded mistress and destitute illegitimate brats accost him at his marriage to Clara, who, in her turn, serves him right by leaving him for another man. The women, too, range from the dried up, amoral and relentlessly calculating Lady Kew, through the economic and religious snobbery of the two banker's wives, to the gentle and beautiful but, from the point of view of conventional people, unfortunately intelligent Ethel Newcome.

As will be discussed in another chapter, the narrative voice of *The Newcomes* belongs to Arthur Pendennis, whose occasional loquaciousness and whose self-righteous, though never strident, wife, Laura, tend to cloy upon modern readers. Pendennis tends to take sides in ways that modern readers object to: he seems to find totally good the naive Colonel, whose rigid indignation and simple-minded notions of right and wrong and of womanly virtue grate rather awkwardly on modern sensibilities. But Pendennis's views are clearly not all shared by the author, and readers should not feel compelled or even impelled to accept them. It is true that Pendennis is the one who said: 'the wicked are wicked no doubt, and they go astray and they fall, and they come by their deserts: but who can measure the mischief which the very virtuous do?'. It is a sentiment repeated in *The Adventures of Philip*, also narrated by Pendennis where he remarks, 'If somebody or some Body of savans[52] would write the history of the harm that has been done in the world by people who believe themselves to be virtuous, what a queer, edifying book it would be, and how poor oppressed rogues might look up! Who burn the Protestants? – the virtuous Catholics, to be sure. Who roast the Catholics? – the virtuous Reformers. Who thinks I am a dangerous character, and avoids me at the club? – The virtuous Squaretoes. Who scorns? who persecutes? who doesn't forgive? – the virtuous Mrs. Grundy.'[53] These are sentiments in which Pendennis and Thackeray both concur as early as *The History of Pendennis*, which is a third-person narration. But, in these later novels, Thackeray has provided a distance between himself and Pendennis that leaves modern readers room to breathe free air and to criticize the narrator's frequently insensitive judgments. *The Newcomes* is the story of a family not unlike other families of its class in England, not unlike Thackeray's own, told from the point of view of a semi-enlightened but still ordinary and conventional narrator, with whom the author and the reader need not always agree.

Finishing *The Newcomes* in June 1855, Thackeray took the next three or four months to write the lectures on the four Georges and prepare himself for a second assault on the United States' dollar in a tour lasting from mid-October to late April and taking him from Buffalo and Boston down the east coast to Charleston and Savannah, over to New Orleans and up the Mississippi and Ohio rivers to St Louis and Cincinnati and back to New York. Again, Thackeray, unlike some of his contemporary British writers, managed to keep back criticisms of Americans' lack of respect for British authors' copyrights, of their pride in the Revolution and their separation from the country he represented, or of their frontier manners – in fact, Thackeray seems genuinely to admire what he took to be American frankness generally, and he clearly was attracted to what he took to be openness and bold honesty in American women.

Upon Thackeray's return from the second lecture tour of America, George Smith made offers for the remaining large serials, but Thackeray remained with Bradbury and Evans for *The Virginians*, the last of his separately published serial novels, because, he explained to Smith, 'my friends Bradbury & Evans have always dealt so honorably by me that I was bound in duty to them'.[54] But the book failed to earn expected profits, and Bradbury and Evans lamented publicly, though not accurately, that they lost money on the book. Thackeray apparently believed it to be true, though an examination of surviving ledgers shows that the publishing house recovered all the investment in materials and labor, all that it paid Thackeray, and made a very small profit – not as much, it is true, as it had hoped. It was in this atmosphere of disappointed hopes that Smith finally wooed Thackeray into a series of contracts to edit the *Cornhill Magazine* and contribute fiction (*Lovel the Widower, Philip* and *Denis Duval*) and editorial essays (*The Roundabout Papers*) to the magazine. And as he had stipulated in 1852 when he signed Thackeray to the *Esmond* contract, George Smith made Thackeray agree not to write for any other publisher while under contract with Smith – which, as it turned out, was the rest of his life. Smith even prevented Thackeray from offering a short piece to *Punch* as a token of reconciliation in 1859.

Early in his career Thackeray had made an unsuccessful bid to be named editor of the *Westminster Review*, and in the mid-1850s he had proposed a periodical to George Smith to be called *Fair Play*, which he withdrew when a chance remark made in praise of his friend and fellow *Punch* contributor, John Leech, blew up in his face. In his enthusiasm for Leech's illustrations, Thackeray said *Punch* would be nothing without them. His other magazine colleagues, of course, took a dim view of the opinion. Thackeray told Smith he could not trust himself to avoid similar blunders, but the truth is, he had other fish to fry; so the idea of editing a magazine was dropped. However, it is not very surprising that Thackeray readily agreed to be editor of the *Cornhill Magazine*, for he believed *The Virginians* was losing money, which he thought proved he was over the hill as a novelist, instead of what in fact it proved: that the publishers had been over-optimistic. *The Virginians* actually sold more copies of its serial form than any previous Thackeray novel; it is just that the publisher had more copies of this book left over than of any previous one.

Editing the *Cornhill*, which began publication in January 1860, made an old dream come true for Thackeray, and Smith kept making offers the author couldn't refuse. In February, April and August, Smith made successive, revised contracts with Thackeray, offering £350 a month for a novel in the first agreement, postponing the new novels in the second one and substituting the *Four Georges* and a short novel, *Lovel*, together worth £1500 in about six months. After that, the novels would begin at £350 a month. And later, Smith added another £1000 a year to have Thackeray as his editor. Then Smith thought to add a monthly essay by Thackeray, *The Roundabout Papers*, so that Thackeray, whose highest monthly income had been £300, with Bradbury and Evans, found himself suddenly receiving as much as £422 a month. Continued negotiations tended to lower both Thackeray's rate of contribution and rate of pay, but he never lacked for money after finding a professional home in the house of Smith, Elder and Company.

Thackeray took his editing duties seriously, agreeing to read all submissions, writing prospectuses and letters of acceptance and rejection, but drawing the line at reading proofs for any but his own writings. Smith and Thackeray agreed not to accept any article without the concurrence of the other, and so there was frequent need for communication. Thackeray did much of the work at home with the help of an amanuensis and a courier for messages to and from Smith's office

*Figure 4.1* Self-portrait in a letter to the publisher, George Smith, lamenting a bad investment, September 1861, *Letters*, IV, 246

and home. The work was onerous and demanding enough to occasion friction between editor and publisher, but the letters show a deep personal regard and respect between the two. Thackeray sponsored Smith's nomination to the Reform Club, and the families exchanged social visits, particularly after Smith's marriage.[55]

Of course, one the first things Thackeray did with his new money was to buy a house, which in short order was completely leveled and rebuilt in the style of Queen Anne, at 2 Palace Green, Kensington, which he and his daughters occupied one year later in March 1861. The purchase was a sort of triumph in Thackeray's restoration of the fortune briefly gained and lost when he was 21. From the publication of *Vanity Fair* he ceased to be a supplicant at publishers' doors for work and pay and became a man of means. But as his wealth improved, his health began to betray him. He suffered from time to time the illnesses to which his age were generally susceptible, including in 1848 a nearly fatal bout of what was probably cholera. But his chronic besetting illness was the recurring attacks of incapacitating pain related to gonorrhea. It is remarkable, when one reads in his letters accounts of being laid up and having to write in bed with a pencil, that he was able to maintain his grueling writing schedule.

Thackeray doted on his daughters and had a special affinity for Anne, whom, he was afraid, even when she was just nine years old, 'would become a man of letters'.[56] His fears did not prevent him employing her as a secretary, her handwriting appearing, when she was 14, in the manuscript *Henry Esmond*. Nor did he stand in the way or take a positive hand when Anne, aged 21, submitted a story anonymously to Smith for the *Cornhill*, and he failed utterly to conceal his pride when Smith, not knowing who the author was, accepted it. Thackeray both feared that Anne and Minnie, whom he at times referred to as Miss Fat and Miss Thin, would be unable to secure husbands and feared that they would. They clearly focused his energies from their birth to his own death, for he frequently said that all his work was aimed at restoring for them his lost patrimony. When his house, furnishings, wine, books and copyrights were sold after his death, on 23 December 1863, each girl had nearly £10000 pounds. Major Carmichael-Smyth died in 1861; Mrs Carmichael-Smyth died in 1864.

# 5
# Reading *Vanity Fair*

When in 1847 William Thackeray set *Vanity Fair* 20–40 years earlier (1810s–30s) and referred casually to actual historical events and persons from the 17th and 18th centuries, his original readers probably recognized a great deal more that was familiar to them from reading newspapers or hearing casual talk at the dinner table than do readers of 2000 or later. To present-day readers such references are likely to be partly obscure and possibly dusty-boring because we no longer know much about the differences in customs, fashions or politics between 1848, 1815 and 1756, nor do we find such differences amusing or surprising – merely quaint. Almost every reader now has a hard time saying or caring when the shift took place in men's fashions from knee breeches to pantaloons or trousers or when the simple clean elegance of the regency buck in the style of Beau Brummel gave way to the flashy and colorful Victorian buck in the style of the Count D'Orsay.[57] And they might have some difficulty in calling to mind the historically true scandal of George the IV's neglect of Francis Rawdon-Hastings or the fact that Hastings was in political opposition to William Pitt (the Younger) and to Henry Dundas, first Viscount Melville.

Thus, when the novelist makes a deft joke or cutting moral commentary in a way that requires such knowledge, most modern readers are befuddled or sail merrily on, oblivious to the point. More importantly, when a reader mistakes the historical condition of character portrayals and narrative voices, curious interpretations may result. Gordon N. Ray, for example, commenting on Amelia Sedley in *Vanity Fair*, chides modern critics for historical naiveté, saying,

'As the nineteenth century drew to a close, and the Victorian heroine (of whom Amelia had come to be regarded as the great prototype and exemplar) fell into disfavor, critics friendly to Thackeray but anxious to bring his books into harmony with the new age hit on a curious theory. Assuming that so intelligent a writer must have shared their own opinions, they interpreted his praise of Amelia as ironical.'[58] He then quotes from a number of critics who tried to 'palliate [Thackeray's] offences against modern taste', concluding that these 'attempts at benevolent exegesis are interesting chiefly as illustrations of the ease with which critics otherwise well-equipped may come a cropper because of their deficiency in historical sense' (p. 36).

All who have worked on Thackeray since the 1940s have a great respect for Gordon Ray and deep appreciation for the quantity and quality of his research and critical assessment of the man and his works. But I was taken aback and struck with the shock of unfamiliarity upon rereading these remarks recently, after having edited *Vanity Fair* and having prepared historical annotations for it,[59] and after developing a deep sense of appreciation for the distanced, bemused, ironic voice of the narrator. I thought I had worked hard to develop a historical sense and keen ear for the narrative voice of the novel, but here is the biographer, the prime historian of Thackeray, speaking of the characters and events in the novel as if Thackeray himself were the narrator and as if the narrative voice could be counted on unironically to represent Thackeray's position, in this case, regarding Amelia, and suggesting that alternative views resulted from a deficiency in historical sense.

I agree completely with Ray's emphasis on the importance of knowledge of history for a discriminating and complex reaction to Thackeray's novel. I disagree, however, both with Ray's assessment of Thackeray's attitude towards Amelia and with his way of speaking about the narrative voice in the novel. It is helpful to learn and keep in mind two ideas in reading *Vanity Fair* simply because so few of us know enough to catch all the jokes. One is that Thackeray's attitude toward Amelia, and indeed all of his major characters, is more complex than Ray seems to suggest. And another is that the narrative voice in *Vanity Fair* is very slippery, indeed.

Even in his own time we find evidence that Thackeray did not necessarily have a partiality for Amelia shared by his contemporaries. Ray himself notes that 'from the first Thackeray's favoritism irritated readers into protest. Miss Rigby wrote contemptuously in the *Quarterly Review* of "the little dolt Amelia," all of whose "philoprogenitive idolatries do not touch us like one fond instinct of 'stupid Rawdon'"' (p. 36). But a rereading of Miss Rigby's review reveals the important point that it was not Thackeray's alleged partiality towards Amelia (which is not mentioned in the review) but Amelia's character itself that irritated the reviewer. In addition, although Thackeray's protean narrator, in some voices, expresses unalloyed approbation of Amelia, in other voices he berates, sneers and laughs at her. For example, he early on claims that 'as we are to see a great deal of Amelia, there is no harm in saying at the outset of our acquaintance that she was one of the best and dearest creatures that ever lived'; but in the revised edition he tones this down to, 'she was a dear little creature'. And in the midst of the ensuing conventional description of this heroine he remarks: 'her face blushed with rosy health, and her lips with the freshest of smiles, and she had a pair of eyes which sparkled with the brightest and honestest good humour except indeed when they filled with tears and that was a great deal too often – for the silly thing would cry over a dead canary-bird or over a mouse that the cat haply had seized upon, or over the end of a novel were it ever so stupid – and as for saying an unkind word to her – were any one hard-hearted enough to do so, – why, so much the worse for them'. (All of which is, however, open to ironic as well as straight interpretation.) He says 'she is not a heroine' because 'her nose was rather short than otherwise, and her cheeks a great deal too round and red' but then refers to Amelia as heroine on five other occasions. Of course he also denies once more that she could be a heroine and once suggested that whether she was or no, we could still treat her as one. On four other occasions he claims Becky is the heroine. And when he wants, the narrator can be quite critical of Amelia as heroine who is referred to as 'a chit' by Becky and by George Osborne's sisters. He remarked at one point:

> Miss Sedley was not of the sun flower sort; and I say it is out of the rules of all proportion to draw a violet of the size of a double-dahlia.
>
> No indeed; the life of a good young girl who is in the paternal nest as yet, can't have many of those thrilling incidents, to which the heroine of romance commonly lays claim.

Most readers detect at least a hint of disdain in the narrator's comment that 'She shook her head sadly, and had, as usual, recourse to the water-works.' Readers also tend to understand why Dobbin:

> is fonder [of his daughter Janey] than of anything in the world – fonder even than of his 'History of the Punjaub.'
>
> 'Fonder than he is of me,' Emmy thinks, with a sigh. (p. 624)

The whole issue becomes interesting and complicated when one realizes that not a one of these narratorial voices is reliable; none can be taken at face value as expressing the thoughts or feelings of the author or (setting authorial intention aside) the values of the book's center of authority.

Thackeray's narrator tends to push responsibility for value judgments on to the reader, but readers might resist accepting this responsibility because they are accustomed to authors who seriously tell readers what to think. So readers need to get to know and trust this author before they feel free to distrust his narrators. In *Vanity Fair* the narrator has no name and is frequently referred to by critics as 'Thackeray', but in later novels there is a named narrator, with a history and character traits clearly distinguishable from Thackeray's. From these novels we can learn something more clearly about the narrative technique. The differences in attitudes toward a woman rather like Amelia are more clearly seen in a passage from *The Newcomes* in which the narrator, Arthur Pendennis (who frequently refers to himself in the third person), listens to George Warrington wax on about the relative merits of the simple Rosey MacKenzie and the aristocratic Ethel Newcome. George tells Pendennis that his wife, Laura:

> believes in that girl [Ethel] whom you all said Clive took a fancy to – before he married his present little placid wife [Rosey], – a nice little simple creature who is worth a dozen Ethels.'
>
> 'Simple certainly,' says Mr. P. with a shrug of the shoulder.
>
> 'A simpleton of twenty is better than a roué of twenty – It is better not to have thought at all than to have thought such things as must go through a girl's mind whose life is passed in jilting and being jilted; whose eyes as soon as they are opened are turned to the main-chance and are taught to leer at an Earl, to languish at a Marquis, and to grow blind before a Commoner.'[60]

Rosey, in this scene, is praised by Warrington in exactly the same tones as those used sometimes by the narrator of *Vanity Fair* and for exactly the same qualities exhibited by Amelia. Yet, Pendennis's shrug and laconic remark reflects the skepticism about Rosey's insipid character that he and his wife Laura have been lamenting for chapters already. Furthermore, few readers of the day lamented for very long the demise of Rosey (though perhaps they should have, not for her endearing qualities as an ideal woman – which she lacked – but for her victimization by an insensitive though handsome husband). They did not lament her because, unlike George Warrington, most readers preferred Ethel as a potential soul mate for Clive.

The voices in *The Newcomes* have names to help keep us from identifying them with the author. But the narrator of *Vanity Fair* has no more illusions about Amelia than Pendennis does of Rosey, and Gordon Ray's mistake, I believe, was not only in equating the author with the narrator but also in taking the narrator's remarks at face value. The slipperiness of the narrative voices in *Vanity Fair* combines with a deft use of history to make a text rich in humor, irony and subtle portrayal of human character. Whether we wish to find out what the author was trying to say or to find out what the author

*Figure 5.1* Self-portrait in letter to a Miss Campbell recommending that she accept the addresses of a young curate of the author's acquaintance, June 1861, *Letters* IV, 240

was trying to hide, one of the most important matters to determine will be whose voice we are hearing in the text and what tone that voice is taking. If we mistake the voice, we will be mistaken about what the text is saying – whether voluntarily or involuntarily.

An analysis of two paragraphs from *Vanity Fair* reveals the demands that book (or rather, its author) makes of readers, and we shall see how all these issues mesh: the problems of history, of text and of reading.

The paragraphs from Chapter VII delineate the genealogy of the Crawley family into which, in 1813, Becky Sharp has come as a governess to Sir Pitt Crawley's two daughters by his second wife. It is useful to remember as well that Thackeray was writing and his original audience were reading these pages in 1847.

In the first paragraph we are introduced to the original 16th-century Crawley who, as a result of entertaining Queen Elizabeth well, was granted the status of borough for his estate and village, and the right to return two representatives to Parliament. His trim beard and good leg invoke images of gentlemen dressed like Sir Walter Raleigh. The fact that the family in the present time of the novel still enjoyed its representatives in Parliament reminds us that the first great Reform Bill would not be passed for another 19 years (in 1832), but denominating the borough 'rotten' indicates that trouble was already brewing.[61] That Sir Pitt did not consider it rotten because it 'produces me a good fifteen hundred a year' reminds us that few if any landowners in those pre-reform years cared for reform.

In the second paragraph we get what appears to be a dry and obscure genealogy:

> Sir Pitt Crawley (named after the great Commoner), was the son of Walpole Crawley, first Baronet, of the Tape and Sealing-Wax Office in the reign of George II., when he was impeached for peculation, as were a great number of other honest gentlemen of those days; and Walpole Crawley was, as need scarcely be said, son of John Churchill Crawley, named after the celebrated military commander of the reign of Queen Anne.

We might analyse this information as follows: Sir Pitt must have been born in the late 1750s or early 1760s when the great Commoner,

William Pitt (the elder), was at the height of his career, for that statesman lost the leadership of his party and accepted a peerage in 1766, losing thereby his appellation as the great Commoner. Sir Pitt Crawley's father, Walpole Crawley, was named for Robert Walpole, who flourished in the 1720s and 1730s and who was opposed in his later years by William Pitt. Walpole Crawley's father, John Churchill Crawley, was named for the great General Marlborough. These are not mere historical facts. A pattern is developing for the naming of Crawley babies: each is named for a leading player in the party currently in power. There is no party loyalty in this family that perpetually crawls to the nearest source of potential favor.

In the next sentence we find that the Crawley who was son of the Crawley of James the First's time is named Charles Stuart Crawley (i.e. named after the king, Charles I). Charles Stuart Crawley very soon exchanged his name for a nickname and became known as Barebones Crawley – a change that must have taken place after Charles I lost his head (1649) and the convening of the Barebones Parilament (1653).

Focusing, however, on the living Crawleys – those who play parts in the novel, set in the 1810s and 1820s, we read as follows:

> Close by the name of Sir Pitt Crawley, Baronet (the subject of the present memoir), are written that of his brother, the Reverend Bute Crawley (the great Commoner was in disgrace when the reverend gentleman was born), ...

It seems then that Pitt and Bute's parents quickly changed their support of William Pitt to John Stuart, third Earl of Bute, who replaced Pitt in the leadership of the party in the mid-1760s, just before their second son was born.

Pitt Crawley, Bute's older brother, of course inherited the title, which explains why Bute went into the Church. Sir Pitt Crawley's first marriage was to the daughter of a fictitious Lord Binkie, but she was a cousin to the real Henry Dundas, first Viscount Melville, a political ally of William Pitt (the younger). Sir Pitt and his wife, Lady Pitt, née Binkie, were even more dexterous in naming their sons than Sir Pitt's father, Walpole Crawley, had been. We read that Lady Binkie:

> brought him two sons: Pitt, named not so much after his father as after the heaven-born minister; and Rawdon Crawley, from the

> Prince of Wales's friend, whom his Majesty George IV. forgot so completely.

The heaven-born minister is William Pitt (the younger) in whose train, Lady Crawley's cousin, Henry Dundas, serves. But Rawdon Crawley is named for Francis Rawdon, later the Marquis of Hastings, who was politically opposed to Pitt and Dundas. Hastings, Governor-General of Bengal from 1812 to 1821, is the friend of the Prince of Wales who was forgotten when the Prince became George IV. The Crawleys are bent as usual upon having it both ways.

None of that, of course, is actually in *Vanity Fair*. Readers, it appears, are just supposed to know it all because it is not just decoration or filler. Although our primary interest in this novel is not all these minor characters and non-characters dragged in by the heels to swell the progress, we learn some valuable facts that help us read the parts of the story that are more obvious, as we shall see.

Our interest at this point is in Becky Sharp who is just entering the Crawley family as a governess. She is to be governess to Sir Pitt's two daughters by his second wife, the daughter of Mr T. Dawson of Mudbury, whom we learn elsewhere is an ironmonger, Sir Pitt having had as much as he could stand of aristocratic women in his first wife, daughter of Lord and Lady Binkie.

The genealogy just rehearsed, allows us to infer, if we just know enough history, that Becky is governess to girls of very little pretension, indeed. Perhaps modern readers would find it gratifying to know that Sir Pitt's title of baronet is the lowest hereditary title in the English system and that his ancestor received the title in exchange for a donation of money – one thousand pounds, to be exact, when titles were being sold in order to raise money for the restoration of Ulster. And more important, as will appear shortly, it should be noted that being a baronet does not make one a peer in England, a designation achieved only at the next rank up, that of baron.

The narrator of *Vanity Fair* then comments about Becky confidentially to the reader:

> It will be seen that the young lady was come into a family of very genteel connexions, and was about to move in a much more distinguished circle than that humble one which she had just quitted in Russell Square.

If nothing else, the word 'humble' used in reference to the excessively proud merchant families of Russell Square, the Sedleys and the Osbornes, should clue the reader in to the ironic tone of voice. But readers who skimmed or skipped the genealogy of the Crawley family, revealing a vulgar, crawling, ne'er-do-well family clinging parasitically to the edges of political power, might think that the narrator, and by extension Thackeray, is guiding their reactions to the story by 'informing them' that the Crawley family is more genteel than the Sedley family rather than pointing ironically at the family's pretensions.

Readers who recognize that the Crawley genealogy is a history of crawling as close to power as possible with next to no success since the initial coup de grace that netted the family two seats in Parliament will also recognize the sly 'misleading' voice of the narrator and will always be on guard against taking anything the narrator says at face value. Even the remark about Walpole Crawley, first Baronet, of the Tape and Sealing-Wax Office in the reign of George II, will be suspect: 'he was impeached for peculation [embezzlement], as were a great number of other honest gentlemen of those days ...'. Honest gentlemen, asks the suspicious reader? We now assume Walpole Crawley was guilty as sin, though we know those gentlemen, like the Keating Five, are honest gentlemen.[62]

Far from being upset at discovering that our narrator has his tongue in his cheek and can never be trusted, perceptive readers see an extraordinary thing taking place. What Thackeray appears to have done is to create a narrator that utterly trusts readers to be intelligent enough, strong enough, witty enough, and confident enough to hold their own in the novel. That narrator never 'dumbs down' to the reader, never assumes the reader didn't get it and has to have it all explained. He in fact is making fun of overly commented novels by offering palpably false comments which the reader can and must reject.

If one does not, however, know enough history, or if one cannot distinguish between various periods in the past, or if one does not trust his or her own judgment and ability to know when the narrator is pulling the reader's leg, one might assume as some critics have that Thackeray is an inconsistent, inept novelist who abdicated his responsibility to provide readers with unambiguous moral judgments on the characters.

Furthermore, one just might miss the meaning of Lord Steyne's remark, 340 pages later, when he hears that Sir Pitt Crawley, his town-house neighbor, has died. 'So that old scoundrel's dead, is he? He might have been a Peer if he had played his cards better. Mr. Pitt had very nearly made him; but he ratted always at the wrong time.' The next rank up from baronet, remember, is baron, the lowest title of the peerage. William Pitt (the younger), for whom Sir Pitt's first born son was named, might have made, perhaps almost did make, Sir Pitt a baron. But no. The wily old baronet named his second son Rawdon, for the opposition, signaling what Lord Steyne called ratting, as usual with the Crawley family, at the wrong time.

That leaves us with another problem. Is the narrator criticizing Sir Pitt for being inept at the game of crawling into greatness? Are we expected to agree with Lord Steyne that Sir Pitt missed his opportunities by not playing his cards right? Or are we to lament the state of worldly affairs that arranges life so that the wicked prosper, unless they are also inept? Are we to lament Sir Pitt in any way? What does the narrator have to say about that? – Well, nothing. The narrator trusts the reader to see the situation and point any moral that fits.

There is, of course, another view to be taken towards all this. In giving the extended genealogy of the Crawley family, Thackeray might have been 'filling up the number', that is, he might have been padding his story so that it would fill the 32-page allotment required by serial publication. Or he might have been mixing history with fiction as part of a larger project to enhance the realism in the novel. Instead of trusting the reader to distrust him, he might have vacillated between commentary on his story that enhances and commentary on his story that merely muddles things.

Two kinds of evidence suggest otherwise: the narrator's own comments on other story-tellers and a series of textual revisions, mostly in the manuscript.

An example of Thackerayan commentary that is quoted by everyone who comments on the novel's narrative technique comes in Chapter VIII, a chapter consisting largely of a letter from Becky Sharp to Amelia Sedley describing Queen's Crawley and its inhabitants in arch, facetious tones that reveal Becky's insincerity, cunning and self-reliance as nothing else has to this point in the novel.

The narrator then comments on Becky's letter: 'Everything considered, I think it is quite as well for our dear Amelia Sedley in Russell

Square, that Miss Sharp and she are parted.' And he quotes bits of Becky's letter to demonstrate that she was a 'droll funny creature' and that she shows 'a great knowledge of the world', and perhaps should have spent the time on her knees during evening prayers 'thinking of something better than Miss Horrocks's ribbons'.

Then, in what some commentators and many readers who did not see through the paragraph on genealogy have taken to be

VANITY FAIR:

PEN AND PENCIL SKETCHES OF ENGLISH SOCIETY.

BY W. M. THACKERAY,

Author of "The Irish Sketch Book:" "Journey from Cornhill to Grand Cairo:" of "Jeames's Diary" and the "Snob Papers" in "Punch:" &c. &c.

LONDON:
PUBLISHED AT THE PUNCH OFFICE, 85, FLEET STREET.
J. MENZIES, EDINBURGH; J. M'LEOD, GLASGOW; J. M'GLASHAN, DUBLIN.
1847.

*Figure 5.2* Self-portrait as narrator clown addressing an audience of clowns, *Vanity Fair*, front wrapper of serialization

Thackeray's own trustworthy voice, the very untrustworthy narrator says:

> But my kind reader will please to remember that these histories in their gaudy yellow covers, have 'Vanity Fair' for a title and that Vanity Fair is a very vain, wicked, foolish place, full of all sorts of humbugs and falsenesses and pretentions. And while the moralist who is holding forth on the cover, (an accurate portrait of your humble servant) professes to wear neither gown nor bands, but only the very same long-eared livery, in which his congregation is arrayed: yet, look you, one is bound to speak the truth as far as one knows it, whether one mounts a cap and bells or a shovel-hat, and a deal of disagreeable matter must come out in the course of such an undertaking.

Readers tend to agree that Vanity Fair is a wicked place, etc. But, says the skeptical reader, since *Vanity Fair,* the book, is in Vanity Fair, the place, does it not also partake in the falsenesses and pretensions of the place? We immediately catch the narrator in a truth, which is a lie, if we think the speaker is Thackeray the trustworthy author. So when this narrator says: 'one is bound to speak the truth as far as one knows it', we may justly suspect that he is hedging – pulling our leg again – rather than alluding merely to every person's limited access to knowledge or truth.

We are confirmed in this suspicion, when in the next two paragraphs he describes first an Italian street story-teller in Naples and then actors on the French stage. In Naples the story-teller joined with his rag-a-muffin audience in responding to the villains of his tale with 'a roar of oaths and execrations against the fictitious monster ... so that the hat went round and the bajocchi tumbled into it in the midst of a perfect storm of sympathy', the story-teller laughing all the way to the bank, so to speak. In the little Paris theatres, the narrator goes on, French actors refuse the parts of vile Englishmen and brutal Cossacks and 'prefer to appear, at a smaller salary, in their real character as loyal Frenchmen'. In both cases, the story-teller, the actors and the audience join in treating the fictions as real. By calling attention to the Italian and French *mistake* of taking fiction for truth, however, the narrator of *Vanity Fair* has re-emphasized that fiction is not real and that *Vanity Fair* is fiction. It is a warning not to fall into the mistake of taking the story at face value.

Ironic insincerity pervades the narrator's next claim 'to show up and trounce his villains…because he has a sincere hatred of them which he cannot keep down, and which must find a vent in suitable abuse and bad language'. Readers know he is pulling their leg, for he has just made fun of the French and Italian audiences for doing what he now pretends to do himself: treat fictional characters as real persons. It seems clear to me that the narrator expects readers to know he is pulling their leg for at least two additional reasons: First, in the next paragraph he says, 'I warn "my kyind friends" then, that I am going to tell…'. The clue is in the quotation marks and spelling of 'my kyind friends' – an echo of the stage manager, Alfred Bunn's, greeting to Drury Lane Theatre audiences. So the narrator, who 'must tell the truth as much as one can', is nothing but a stage manager. Indeed, he never seriously pretended to be anything other than that – as he declares in his preface, significantly titled 'Before the Curtain'.

And in the next paragraph the narrator says, 'And as we bring our characters forward, I will ask leave as a man and a brother not only to introduce them, but occasionally to step down from the platform and talk about them.' Again our wary, suspicious reader refuses to believe this is the author, Thackeray, speaking in his own voice about his narrative method, for the phrase 'as a man and a brother' triggers the odd sensation that he has just adopted the persona of a black man and slave. The phrase 'Am I not a man and a brother' is the slogan of the English abolitionist movement and appears on their medallion of a Negro slave in chains. The narrator 'as a man and a brother', then, asks the reader (his master?) leave to comment on the characters throughout the book.

The second major argument supporting the idea that Thackeray deliberately trusts the reader to point the moral of his tale is found in textual revisions. Even with the evidence already cited, one could remain skeptical of the assertion that the narrator is deliberately refusing to load the dice one way or another – skeptical of the idea that the author systematically trusts the reader to distrust the narrator systematically. One could still conclude that the author was inept or just ambiguous unintentionally. But the following evidence suggests otherwise.

When Sir Pitt, in chapter X, tells his son, Pitt, not to 'preachify' while Miss Crawley, the wealthy spinster aunt, is visiting, the first version in the manuscript reads:

> 'Why, hang it, Pitt,' said the father to his remonstrance. 'You wouldn't be such a flat[63] as to let three thousand a year go out of the family?'
>
> 'What is money compared to our souls, Sir?' continued Crawley *who knew he was not to inherit a shilling of his aunt's money*. [italics added]

The last phrase, in the narrator's voice, 'who knew he was not to inherit a shilling of his aunt's money' was canceled. The accusation instead becomes Sir Pitt's, who says: 'You mean that the old lady won't leave the money to you.' However, after the father's retort, the manuscript revision continued in the narrator's voice, to make a bald assertion about the characters:

> 'You mean that the old lady won't leave the money to you' – *this was in fact the meaning of Mr. Crawley. No man for his own interest could accommodate himself to circumstances more. In London he would let a great man talk and laugh and be as wicked as he liked: but as he could get no good from Miss Crawley's money why compromise his conscience?. This was another reason why he should hate Rawdon Crawley. He thought his brother robbed him. Elder brothers often do think so; and curse the conspiracy of the younger children wh. unjustly deprives them of their fortune*. [italics added]

This unmistakable commentary, telling the reader the exact moral standing of both father and son, is then also canceled in favor of a musingly ambiguous question. In proof the passage appeared as follows:

> 'You mean that the old lady won't leave the money to you' – and who knows but it was Mr. Crawley's meaning?

When the last version appeared in proof, someone (probably Thackeray) drove the doubtfulness home by adding italics to *was*: 'and who knows but it *was* Mr. Crawley's meaning?'. The effect is to cast additional doubt on the narrator's overt statement and to intensify the suspicion that both Crawleys are corrupt to the core.

Can there be any question about Thackeray's deliberate intention to push onto readers the responsibility for pointing morals and judging the characters?

Another example of the author's control over the narrative tone might cement the idea that Thackeray was trusting his readers to draw their own conclusions. The Waterloo Battle in chapter 32 of *Vanity Fair* comes to a close with this paragraph:

> No more firing was heard at Brussels – the pursuit rolled miles away. The darkness came down on the field and city, and Amelia was praying for George, who was lying on his face, dead, with a bullet through his heart.

The effect on many readers has been thrilling and chilling, as they are forced through the opposing passions generated by the sorrow for sudden death and for poor Amelia who does not participate at all in the pleasure of seeing George dead. In fact, however, the passage says nothing about sorrow or pleasure; for the language is crisp, clean, efficient, and flat. There is no suggestion that Amelia is shedding tears over what Becky in chapter 67 will call with great justice a selfish humbug, a low-bred cockney-dandy, and a padded booby. The mere facts here are supposed to carry a great deal of emotional freight.

What did Thackeray, as opposed to the narrator, think about George and his death? Well, outside the novel he expressed himself at least twice. Two months before this passage was published, he responded to his mother's criticism of Amelia as being selfish with some general remarks about greed generally in Vanity Fair and the rarity of humility, and then he added: 'Amelia's [humiliation] is to come, when her scoundrel of a husband is well dead with a ball in his odious bowels…'.[64] There is nothing flat or neutral in that version of George's death. Nine months after the passage was published, Thackeray wrote in an entirely different mood to a Miss Smith, declining a dinner invitation on the grounds that it was the 'Hannawussary of the death of my dear friend Captain George Osborne of the –th regiment.' The letter is decorated with a cartoon battle scene of cannon, soldiers, Napoleon escaping on a horse

('Bony runnin away like anythink'), and, lying face down, 'Capting Hosbin ded a bullick through his Art.'[65]

At the very least Thackeray the person had no qualms about expressing his opinion of George to his correspondents, but in the novel the narrator tends to be ambiguous or neutral just when the temptation is great to intrude and point the moral of the story. Recognizing this control might make the reader look for other subtleties in the text. Readers of the first edition could note, for example, that the last sentence of that paragraph closing chapter 32 begins with the phrase, 'The darkness came down' while readers of the revised edition would read, 'Darkness came down.' Both indicate the time of day and both suggest, perhaps, that a greater, symbolic, darkness descended that day. But readers who note that Thackeray took the trouble to remove the opening article, might be even more inclined to think that 'Darkness' with a capital D now starts that last sentence; a personified Darkness has descended on the day and on the book. And remember, this is the end of a monthly installment; original readers had to wait 30 days for the next chapter.

Readers of *Vanity Fair* confront a difficult task. Unassisted, they might collapse history into two segments: Now, and long ago; for some readers the differences between now and 1986 are more palpable and real than those between 1756 and 1848. Unassisted they might also collapse the voices from the fiction into one category: The Author; for many have been 'trained' in school to find a bit of biographical information to give a sense of who is speaking. For some readers distinguishing between author and narrator is a new idea and distinguishing between straight and ironic narration is something they think was invented by stand-up comics on television. Unassisted they might, furthermore, collapse history and fiction into one segment: Fiction, not recognizing Bute and Pitt and Dundas and Hastings as historical figures or not knowing which is fiction and which fact when confronted by the Groom of the Bedchamber and the Baronet of the Tape and Sealing Wax Office.

Knowing the difference between the fictional references and the historical, knowing the difference between the various periods of history, knowing the biography and appearance of the author and the fictitious biography and appearance of the narrator, knowing the market-place for literature in which it made sense to publish a novel in 32-page pamphlets with yellow covers – knowing all these things makes it possible to make discriminations about the tone of voice we are hearing as we read and makes a great, long, boring book into an exciting, penetrating, troubling book that reveals human foibles from the days of the first Queen Elizabeth to those of the second.

# 6
# Thackeray's Women

Becky Sharp is, possibly, the most famous female character from Victorian fiction. She would at least be included in any list that named Jane Eyre, Dorothea Brooke, Catherine Earnshaw and Esther Summerson.[66] Becky is one kind of Thackerayan woman, similar to Beatrix Esmond, Blanche Amory, and even Ethel Newcome in being intelligent, headstrong and wily. These beautiful, accomplished, manipulative, calculating women stand out primarily because they run counter to the more commonly admired women of Victorian fiction of whom Amelia Sedley has been called the epitome: the reticent, retiring, subservient, helpless Victorian heroine. I think it a mistake, however, to think of Thackeray's women in stereotypical terms. His portraits are highly individualized. Furthermore, his understanding of the limits placed by society on women's choices, and his sympathy for their forced position in society and for their conventionalized powerlessness is matched by his understanding of the means available to women to redress their own condition within the conventions that limited them.

There are three interlocked strands of Thackeray's thought that I think are needed in order to see how Thackeray's portraits of women work. The first and most important is his relationships with women at every level in his life, particularly his relationships with his daughters whose welfare rested on his shoulders alone from their births in 1837 and 1840 until his death. They were the one relationship with women he never escaped. The second is his philosophical and religious development, the cast of his mind which affected his humor, his sympathies and the writing style used to raise sensitive issues. The third is his financial condition and his desire to leave his daughters at least as well off as he had been – to restore the patrimony he had lost. Weaving these three strands is the burden of this chapter.

The depths of emotional betrayal suffered by Thackeray's mother when her grandmother lied about the death of Ensign Carmichael-Smyth must have been conveyed to Thackeray at some time in his youth, for his fiction frequently portrays the machinations of parents and guardians in their attempts to arrange for the 'proper' marital bliss of children. But for Thackeray it is always a complex relation, for parents can be 'right' – as proved the case in *Pendennis*, where Arthur, romantic young fool that he was, lost his heart to the stage presence of an actress 10 years his senior and of no education or talents except the ape-like one of imitation instilled by her tutor, Mr Bows.

Having recovered from the heady, hormonal, Byronic throes of first love, Pendennis is grateful to his uncle and mother, who had been his enemies in love. Pen's mother has been described by one enthusiastic critic as Thackeray's wickedest woman, for her love could be tyrannical, disapproving of every independent move, whenever possible controlling both Pen and Laura and triumphing in her deathbed wish that they be married. She wins. This may be too harsh a judgment of Helen Pendennis, but it suggests the pattern of behaviour between Thackeray and his mother Anne. Throughout her life she expressed her opinions on his way of living. Deeply supportive, she kept his daughters for him from the time of their mother's illness in 1840 until Thackeray reached a level of financial security in 1846 that allowed him to have a house and a household staff sufficient to keep the children with him. She also kept them during his tours of the United States. But she drove both the son and the granddaughters to near distraction with her insistent advice about medicine for the body and dogma for the soul. Furthermore, at her insistence Thackeray scrapped the original chapter on Jerusalem in *Notes on a Journey from Cornhill to Grand Cairo* – the content of which is suggested by two letters to his mother at the time:

> I am gravelled with Jerusalem, not wishing to offend the public by a needless exhibition of heterodoxy: not daring to be a hypocrite.

> I have been reading lots of books – Old Testament: Church Histories: Travels and advance but slowly in the labour. I find there was a sect in the early Church who denounced the Old Testament: and get into such a rage myself when reading all that murder and crime wh. the name of the Almighty is blasphemously made to Sanction: that I don't dare to trust myself to write, and put off my work from day to day.[67]

A few days later he responded to his mother's advice:

> My dearest Mammy. I'm sure your advice is quite right – I'm not going to preach heterodoxy: I cant be hypocritical however, wh. surely is a much greater sin against God. We don't know what orthodoxy is indeed. Your orthodoxy is not your neighbour's – Your opinion is personal to you as much as your eyes or your nose or the tone of your voice. ... But the Great Intelligence shines far far above all mothers and all sons – the Truth Absolute is God – And it seems to me hence almost blasphemous: that any blind prejudiced sinful mortal being should dare to be unhappy about the belief of another; should dare to say Lo I am right and my brothers must go to damnation ...[68]

In that letter Thackeray first articulates his rejection of the Old Testament in terms very similar to those he used 10 years later in a renewal of the argument in an exchange of letters between Thackeray, his mother and his daughter. They demonstrate the complexity of their relationships, showing that the mother in fact tried hard to be fair, that the son rebelled with a broken heart, and that somehow the daughter grew emotionally healthy and mentally strong. In September 1852, when Anne, just 15, was left with her grandmother while Thackeray prepared for his first tour of the United States, his mother wrote:

> And now to come to the painful difference that alas! & alas is come between us – If the dear children were not with me, I would shut it up & and only refer to it in my prayers – but they are here, they are under my teaching & that teaching must be fr[o]m what I believe it to be the 'word of GOD' – I must dwell upon every passage that more particularly assures the believer of the promises made to him – As for instance in our reading yesterday

> we left off at the 36th v. of 10 c of John, & at the 35th v: I said 'remember children & write it in yr hearts & may God keep it there – that it is the word of God['] & that 'the Scripture cannot be broken' – it is our Lord himself who speaks – My conscience says I can do no other, but it also says you are condemning their Father, & it is an infinite pain to me – It seems to me that the difference between us is just this, you put them to sea without a compass & pointing to a star, tell them they are to keep it before them & that they will arrive at it – however I am not going into the subject – My honest purpose is to show you that I cannot have them with me, without teaching them, that 'all Scripture is given by inspiration fr[o]m GOD,['] & that as children they must know the Holy Scriptures, that 'are able to make them wise unto salvation' – I would rather take St Paul's authority in this last quotation than anything you or any Man can say – the conflict is a very severe one between the two duties – not fr[o]m a moments doubt in my own mind, but fr[o]m the great pain of implying to them ever that you are wrong – The work will not be mine if they are brought to recognize the truth of God's word – poor Nanny's is a stiff heart of unbelief, & it came upon me like a thunderbolt when I heard her declare that she 'did not care for the old Testament & considered the new only historical' – it was tremendous to hear such words, & my only consolation is that she can give no reason for her unbelief, –[69]

However, Mrs Carmichael-Smyth did not mail the letter in September when she wrote it, though it is clear that similar sentiments were expressed in now lost correspondence. In fact, the following letters were sent before she added a coda and mailed the September letter to Thackeray in New York in January. In the meantime in mid-October Thackeray wrote in a remarkably frank style to young Anne:

> I should read all the books that Granny wishes, if I were you: and you must come to your own deductions about them as every honest man and woman must and does. When I was your age I was accustomed to hear and read a great deal of the Evangelical (so called) doctrine and got an extreme distaste [Thackeray crossed out but left legible 'and contempt'] for that sort of

composition ... Daubigne I believe is the best man of the modern French Reformers: and a worse guide to historical truth (for one who has a reputation) I dont know – if M. Gossaint argues that because our Lord quotes the Hebrew Scriptures therefore the Scriptures are of direct divine composition: you may make yourself quite easy; and the works of a reasoner who would maintain an argument so monstrous need not I should think occupy a great portion of your time. Our Lord not only quoted the Hebrew writings ... but he contradicted the Old Scriptures flatly ...

And the misfortune of dogmatic belief is that the first principle granted that the Book called the Bible is written under the direct dictations of god ... [is that] pain, cruelty, persecution, separation of dear relatives, follow as a matter of course. ... Did you hear the Chapter of the Sunday before last about Jehu murdering the Priests of Baal? The Lord says Cut away Jehu, the Lord says Murder them Jehu Smite smash run them through the body Kill 'em old and young – Do you believe the Lord directly gave any such orders: or that a chief of an Eastern race, devout, alone, worshipping one God, and finding his people perverted by idolators his neighbours determined to make an end of his enemy by slaughtering the priests who led them. The Lord ordered Robespierre to set the guillotine up a Jehu Napoleon to slaughter the people before St Roch just in the same way – And you may read the Hebrew scriptures rationally or literally as you like. To my mind Scriptures only means a writing and Bible means a Book. It contains Divine Truths: and the history of a Divine Character; but imperfect but not containing a thousandth part of Him ...[70]

On 5 December, Anne wrote her father a long newsy letter with the following concluding paragraph:

I am afraid Grannie is still miserable about me, but it bothers me when the clergymen say that everybody ought to think alike and follow the one true way, forgetting that it is they who want people to think alike, that is, as they do. Monsieur Monod [the family's spiritual leader at the time] tells us things about the Garden of Eden, which he proves by St. Paul's epistles. I don't understand how God can repent and destroy His own work, or how He can make coats as He did for Adam, or shut a door, as

> they say He shut Noah in, and it is things like these that they think one must go to hell for not respecting and believing. I am sure when Christ talks about 'My words' He means His own, not the Bible, as Grannie says, but I don't know what it means when He says that He did not come to destroy the law but to fulfil it, and so I suppose everybody is right and nobody knows anything. Minnie and I can love you and Grannie with all our heart, and that is our business.[71]

Mail traveled slowly but Thackeray received the letter in early January and on the 5th wrote to his mother:

> I must write you a line, and kiss my dearest old Mother, though we differ ever so much about the Old Testament. What a deal of heart-burning & unkindness what division between friends has that book caused! – It can't be otherwise with your views regarding it, what can you do but deplore the error of those who won't receive it – what can I, but say my say too, & trust in God if I'm wrong – Trust if I'm wrong? It would be mistrust & a sort of Atheism in me to doubt for a moment that He will be good to me and all creatures – and if I kneel down and pray to God with my children, I must tell them too as reverently & carefully as I can what my views are upon this most awful of all subjects – It wasn't I that taught Nanny to beat her little hands on the picture of Abraham and Isaac. I wish that we could have the comfort of believing together: but, in all opinion, we are made different: and I must follow my truth though it's not my dear old Mother's – with this advantage over you that my conviction leads me to no sorrow or distrust about yours; You don't like the people I like nor the opinions I like nor the books I like – I don't like what you like – Ah me – our minds are no more alike than our noses: and each must follow his own. I wouldn't have the children whilst with you go to other than your church: but seeing you uncomfortable about Anny & poor Nan unhappy that you are so (a word from each is enough to show me what is going on) I can't help myself, but must speak my mind. I wouldn't have the girls Lovatites or belonging to that sect of Xtians because I dont think their doctrine is a true one – and when I find they are sitting under a Calvinist Doctor with the dear old Granny fondly urging his truths on them – Doctor Papa must say his sermon (whose

> happiness in life depends on what you are doing but that is nothing if it's true you *must* do it and you think it true) – and may God Almighty teach them the right way. I wrote Private on that letter to Anny[72] wh. hurt you – I meant you not to read it: not that I want to keep secrets from you but simply not to talk about a subject on wh. I must speak and we can't agree. And I know that in talking so there will be an occasion for fresh tears and pain – If I were to talk with GP about the 3 angles of a triangle we might differ but we shouldn't grieve – I cant help myself with you – the question of reason becomes one of sentiment straightway: and you suffer pangs (and inflict them too) about what is a calculation, like the 3 angles of a triangle, of evidence probability & so forth. Parents have been made unhappy, children parted from them, people have killed persecuted been killed and persecuted in all ages upon this question – We can't help it coming not as peace but a sword into our family. And mine must go, with me for Chief Magistrate, God help us – and we must take the truth and its consequences sweet & bitter – Of course I am unhappy, and you knew I would not like it that my children should be sitting under a French Calvinist – but his views being yours it was your duty to pursue them in spite of me: and to bind me down on the Altar whether I would or no. But I must speak too and whenever I hear of these things speak I will. Assez.[73]

No doubt this defense of himself and his children from the zeal of his mother prompted her to complete on 20 January the letter started in September:

> It is 4 months since this was written & you may find some assurance of the children's faith in you when I tell you that they wd. think it a crime to think otherwise than as you have told them – & so firmly am I convinced that *I can* do nothing, that I have ceased for some time to read the Scriptures with them, they taking them as the word of Man & upon Man's word called to believe the most stupendous of mysteries, *I firmly* believing them to be the word of GOD, read with so different a spirit that nothing good could arise fr[o]m the communion. I have begged them to read the Bible daily.

It is not hard to see in the grandmother's despair a continued criticism of the son. Hers was a righteous and possessive love, and

Thackeray learned to portray it in his women characters, especially Helen and Laura, but also in wives like Amelia in *Vanity Fair* and Rosey in *The Newcomes*, who control their men by love.

Perhaps the more important point to be made about this intersection of family ties and religious beliefs is that Thackeray's doubts in religious matters extended to, or were an extension of, his ability to see more than one side of most issues and to detect the logical gaps in defenses of favorite ideas. Thus, he adopted both a tentative sympathy and mild distrust in his treatment of all persons whose beliefs or behaviours may have departed from expected norms. He was not averse to expressing his opinions, but he refused to force them onto others, and he resisted the fashion of his time to express righteous indignation or to ally himself with righteous causes. The effect of doubt was a gentle tolerance and a willingness to see circumstances and moral imperatives from the point of view of his characters rather than from an *a priori* principled position.

That did not, of course, sit well with some of his contemporaries, who like Anthony Trollope wished Thackeray were more forceful. This characteristic of Thackeray's, to withhold judgment, to be more inquisitive and less judgmental, marks perhaps the most profound difference between him and his more popular contemporary Charles Dickens, who never seemed to hesitate when declaring a character to be a villain or an innocent. Dickens' surefootedness in moral matters in his novels, regardless of the moral ambiguities of his own life, satisfies many readers' desire for guidance. Thackeray's tolerance for difference and understanding of moral weakness was combined with a narrative technique that put the burden of judgment on the reader – a burden some readers refuse to accept. Thackeray requires readers who can guide themselves – the basic argument of Chapter 5 in this book. And the reason, I believe, lies not only in the religious skepticism arising from the play of common sense and the philosophical acceptance of an uncertainty principle but also in the delicate relations between an overzealous mother, a skeptical son and an inquisitive and loving daughter.

As can be seen in his fiction, Thackeray's experiences with women engendered sympathy with and tolerance for views other than his own and other than the conventional views often associated with Victorians. To follow Pendennis's women is to follow a track parallel to Thackeray's women. The lesson of a nearly disastrous first love did not prevent Arthur Pendennis from launching forthwith into a mock romantic attachment with Blanche Amory, who was an actress in her own right, playing at love and at all of life's domestic and social roles where scarcely any of her moves were uncalculated or unrehearsed. And, having escaped the gloomy falsity of love with Blanche, Arthur encourages an affair of the opposite kind with Fanny Bolton, a poor porter's daughter. With no apparent artifice or defense against artifice, Fanny appears to fall deeply in love with Arthur whose sole motive was to amuse himself by playing the gentle gallant – a role he was incapable of controlling. Saved by illness and a high-handed, high-minded and suspicious mother, Arthur avoids a disastrous match with Bolton – who, for all her tender devotion to Pen and her apparent naiveté, consoled herself rather quickly by marrying Sam Huxter.

*Figure 6.1* Woodcut of Pendennis fishing for Blanche Amory, *Pendennis*, I, 223

Following the demands of fiction, Arthur's true love eventually appears, as he finds a perfect partner in none other than his surrogate sister, the orphaned Laura, a woman without dissimulation, without guile, and without pretense – but with a rather strong sense of right and dignity and propriety that cloys on most readers. Perhaps that is why Thackeray chose to name her after London's notorious reigning queen of whoredom, Laura Bell. Laura was the result of another 'sad' love story involving Helen Pendennis's first love, another aborted affair. Helen Thistlewood had fallen in love with her cousin, Francis Bell, who unfortunately was inextricably engaged to his first love, a woman 10 years his senior. It is a story that Arthur's father never permitted to be mentioned even though he did allow Laura to be raised in his home. Francis Bell, followed by his aged wife (10 years often seem longer in fiction than in life), took a posting to Coventry Island where his harridan fell ill and died. By this time Helen had married, too, so Francis took a new wife who was Laura's mother. He soon died also, recommending his daughter to his true but inaccessible love, Helen Thistlewood Pendennis, who raised Laura implicitly for her son Pen.

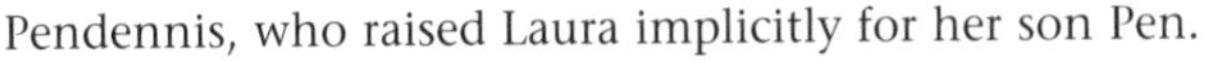

*Figure 6.2* Vignette for ch. 10, in which Pendennis plays Sir Lancelot to Fanny Bolton's Lady of Shalott, *Pendennis*, II, 97

This story combines several elements in Thackeray's family history. The love story derives in part from the matches opposed as unsuitable by parents – like Anne Becher's with Henry Carmichael-Smyth or Thackeray's own with Isabella Shaw – and, perhaps, in part from the escaped mismatches in Thackeray's youth already suggested. But the orphaned Laura seems a fictional rendition of Thackeray's cousin, Mary Eliot Graham, the daughter of his maternal aunt who had accompanied his mother to India in search of a husband. When her parents both died, Mary came to live with the Carmichael-Smyths and was, of course, there, every time Thackeray came home from school for holidays. There is no evidence that his mother, like Pen's, wanted the two to marry, and, in fact, Mary Graham eventually married Charles Carmichael-Smyth, Thackeray's stepfather's younger brother.

*Figure 6.3* Vignette for ch. 16, in which Fanny Bolton's reputation is invented by her detractors, *Pendennis*, II, 151

In his own life Thackeray never found Laura. He, too, lost his heart (and apparently his virginity) to a French governess met at a masquerade party in Paris while on a clandestine holiday from college. She was, of course, 10 years older than Thackeray, but we do not know the particulars or how he extracted himself from so unpromising a liaison. How many love affairs the young Thackeray enjoyed and suffered through before his wedding, there is no way to tell.

But Thackeray understood the business of novel writing to be that of telling love stories, and he transmogrified at least some of his own experiences into his novels. In his mid- and late 40s he made fun of himself as an aging gentleman still trying to write the lives of youngsters falling in love – or playing at falling in love. But the fact is, Thackeray never stopped that game himself.

The happy times of his marriage to Isabella Shaw had lasted at most four years. For four more years he alternated between putting her in the care of doctors and trying to care for and nurse her at home. Mary Graham helped with Isabella's care, as did a neighbour, Mrs Procter, to whose husband Thackeray eventually dedicated *Vanity Fair*. But by late 1845, Isabella's incurable condition and final placement with a family in Camberwell left Thackeray a *de facto* widower, with two young daughters to raise. British law recognized no grounds for divorce in his situation, as is well known from Rochester's similar condition in Charlotte Brontë's *Jane Eyre*. Unable to remarry, and living in a society that was increasingly circumspect about irregular relationships between men and women, his contacts with women were apparently chaste and often epistolary. We, of course, do not know what physical relations he had with women – prostitutes, perhaps – of whom one did not write. He had obviously had such relationships before his marriage, but after his 'widowhood' there are no diary entries hinting at any such escapades.

In a study everyone interested in Victorian life and letters either has or should read, *The Novels of the Eighteen Forties*, Kathleen Tillotson traces the parallel development of increased prudery in novels and public life from the 1830s to the 1850s, a study that helps modern readers greatly in understanding how to read the novels of the time, especially a work like *Vanity Fair*. But it would be a mistake, I think, to suggest that Thackeray's conjugal rectitude or the intense restraint on his emotional life was dictated by the narrowing moral conventions of the time. It is true that he enjoyed the social life of London and that overt affairs, or even one affair, would have cost him the entrée to most respectable London houses. Witness the effect on George Eliot's life when she took up a monogamous relation with George Lewes, who was married though separated from a woman known to be the mistress of another man. Witness the effect on the social life of J.S. Mill when he dallied round the Taylor household until the husband died and then married the widow. Witness the scandal of John Ruskin's marriage and annulment with Effie Grey, and of George Meredith's marriage to Ellen Peacock who abandoned him for a painter. Obviously unconventional liaisons did take place in London among Thackeray's contemporaries, though such events and connections exacted a high social price. Had Thackeray been without children, as was true in every one of the famous cases just mentioned, his story might have been different. But he was a father who cared deeply for his children and their welfare. And though it is widely thought that his was a temperament that needed a woman, his letters frequently mention his various duties to his children – not just his need to restore to them the inheritance that he had lost but his need to provide them with a home, love and appropriate education. An open scandal was not an option for him as it was for many of the writers and painters and aristocrats, too, whom he knew.

His letters show that he developed an extraordinary number of confidential relationships with women who were emotional supports to him. In 1846, while writing *Vanity Fair* at a hotel in Brighton, he met Kate Perry with whom, according to comments written by her after Thackeray's death, a great friendship sprang up over night. Kate lived with a married sister Jane Elliot in a house frequently open to a circle of writers, philosophers and friends that included Thackeray and his college friends William Brookfield, George Venables, James Spedding and others such as Lord Houghton. But in the Perry sisters, Thackeray found confidantes with whom for the rest of his life he shared the secret loves of his life, and especially his love for Jane Brookfield, wife of his good friend William. Thackeray leaned upon the sisters for emotional support, particularly when the Brookfield affair went awry, and they appear to have given him the support he needed.

At least twice Thackeray's friendships with women took a significant toll on his heart: with Jane Brookfield whom he first met in 1842 and from whose society he was banned in 1851; and with Sally Baxter, an American girl 20 years his junior whom he met in 1852 and who married into a famous South Carolinian family in 1855. The friendship with Jane Brookfield, the wife of his best friend, began naturally enough. Thackeray was still dealing desperately with Isabella's illness and Jane was a partial invalid who seems to have confided in Thackeray some doubts about her husband, a man

11 years her senior. By 1848 when Thackeray was deep into the writing of *Pendennis*, he had become emotionally dependent on Jane, and he came to believe that his love for her was returned. Yet William Brookfield was his friend, and propriety demanded an innocent framework for any correspondence or converse between Jane and Thackeray. The fiction they chose was to describe their affection for one another as that of a brother and sister – nothing more than a deep friendship and mutual admiration. But while this strategy maintained a respectable face on what was troubling at least Thackeray's heart, it exacerbated the frustration, for it amounted to a lie they told each other as well as the world. Whether by accident or connivance, Jane and Thackeray were together unchaperoned on a train trip from London to Clevedon Court, Jane's family's home, and it was while on that visit that it is just possible that the relationship became more than the platonic affair it was supposed to be. Readers of *The Newcomes* will recognize this episode in the train trip Clive and Ethel take to Brighton and the uproar and indignation vented upon the young man by his Aunt Honeyman for his duplicity and for what might have happened while the train passed through a tunnel.

Though much of their correspondence was destroyed and what remains has been freely snipped and overscored, it is clear that the 'brother/sister' love under which Jane and Thackeray conducted their relationship came to rankle with Jane's husband from whom the pair of friends believed – or at least claimed – they had nothing to hide. When Brookfield let his pent-up irritation against his wife spill over in Thackeray's presence one evening in September 1851, Thackeray in some surprise and chagrin rebuked the husband after which they were friends no longer, and William Brookfield barred Thackeray from further visits to Jane. Thackeray's aggrieved innocence found vent in a remarkable correspondence with Kate Perry and Jane Elliot, who we can be pretty sure relayed its contents to Jane Brookfield. And he nursed his bruised ego vicariously in the narrative history of *Henry Esmond*, which he had just begun to write, chronicling the demise of the loveless marriage of Frank and Rachel Castlewood and making clear that Rachel's love for Esmond, though heavily veiled, preceded her husband's death. Thackeray may have indulged a modicum of revenge against Jane by having Esmond transfer his love from Rachel onto her daughter Beatrix, a 'betrayal'

Rachel perforce suffered in silence. There is no surviving evidence to indicate how deeply Jane Brookfield felt the separation from Thackeray. It is possible that she was far more passive in the relationship than Thackeray wished to believe. He was shocked and aggrieved to hear she was pregnant, for he took it as evidence that the relationship between Jane and her husband was other than he had been led to believe.

Be that as it may, the emotional trauma of the Brookfield relationship, like that of his wife's mental breakdown, left Thackeray not only more melancholy but also wiser and tenderer in his understanding of both men and women and of their thwarted desires. Thackeray's indignation against prudes and disciplinarians in his fiction, his sympathy with young love and the innocent pleasures of the theater and light fiction, and his delight in the laughter of children all stem from his own experiences in lost opportunities for joy.

Having written out his anger and hurt in *Esmond*, Thackeray undertook in October 1852 a lecture tour of the United States, talking about the eighteenth century writers he loved most and about Jonathan Swift, whom he included as an accomplished writer and a student of the 'humours' but in whose personality and point of view he found little to admire. The tour took him from New York to Boston and then south to Savannah with stops in Richmond, Washington and other cultural centers. While in New York, he struck up a friendship with George Baxter in whose home Thackeray found a congenial family and comfort. He sought the Baxters' society often during his stay in New York, perhaps because of the beautiful, imperious, fascinating Sally, aged 18.

The relationship with Sally Baxter was playful, though Thackeray wrote his mother, to whom he confessed the oddest things, of his surprise and pleasure in discovering that even at his age the foolish emotions of young love were still available to him. He was 41 years old. Again there was a long correspondence, all tightly controlled in its expressions of affection. And the renewal of acquaintance upon Thackeray's second visit to the United States must have been touching because Sally was about to be married to Frank Wade Hampton of South Carolina. Though invited to attend the ceremony Thackeray avoided it, apparently because of real, though of course unjustified, feelings of envy. Thackeray's confidantes included Mrs Anne Procter, who had been a principal support to him in his troubles with

Isabella and to whose husband Bryan 'Barry Cornwall' Procter, he dedicated *Vanity Fair*. And, of course Jane Elliot and Kate Perry had full accounts from the author of the workings of his silly old heart. Thackeray's correspondence with Sally Baxter Hampton continued until 1861, when the Civil War had separated her from her family in New York and she died, aged 27, of consumption in a strange land though in the arms of a devoted husband.[74]

But it is not just these emotionally violent relapses into young love – the passions of a beating heart that suspend judgment and decorum and which in Thackeray's novels are treated both tenderly and ironically – not just 'love affairs' that demonstrated Thackeray's desire for and dependence on women. In addition to his close confidantes like the Perry sisters, and Mrs Procter, his acquaintances included women of some public note like Mrs Gore, Lady Blessington, and Mrs Caroline Norton, aristocrats like Lady Ashburton and Lady Stanley, literary wives like Jane Carlyle, and dinner hostesses about whose relationships with Thackeray we know little or nothing and for which there is no reason to suspect intimacy of any sort. But these others are to be understood, I believe, in a light not available either to normally married men, regardless of their unfaithfulness to their wives, or to 'confirmed bachelors' who were so by choice or (usually suppressed) sexual orientation.

Thackeray was, sexually, a vigorous male with the social aspirations and reticence of an upper middle-class, classically educated, Victorian man. He fit comfortably into the world of men, who at stag dinners, such as the weekly *Punch* dinners engaged in bawdy talk. Although he records his disgust at a 'common brothel' to which William Maginn, his editor at *Fraser's Magazine* had taken him four years before his marriage, his sexual drives clearly overcame any moral or social resistance to illicit sex. Furthermore, the humor of his early writing derives in no small part from a 'manly' enjoyment of stereotypically manly appetites for drink and male companionship and 'wild nights'.

Of these other women in Thackeray's life, one of the most remarkable was Caroline Norton. Two years Thackeray's senior, she was from a poor family of seven children, and though beautiful, intelligent and head strong, had married George Norton at age 19 'for practical reasons'. Within four years she had attracted the attentions of William Lamb, Lord Melbourne, who secured a lucrative sinecure for George Norton, which he enjoyed for life. However, in 1836, when the family had increased by three children, George Norton lost his patience with Lord Melbourne and brought a crim. con. (criminal conversation or adultery) charge against him. Though he lost the suit, the battle was pitched with his wife, who claimed actual innocence as well as legal acquittal. For the next 20 years at least, Caroline Norton wrote pamphlets and public letters on behalf of married women's rights, child custody laws, and separation and divorce laws and against the double standard of morality that inhered in all such laws in England at the time. As a married woman, her children, her property, her gifts from Lord Melbourne and her earnings from writing all belonged by law to her violent and abusive husband, George Norton. But she was a charming, fascinating and social woman who had extensive entrée in the fashionable world of London where she lobbied personally with lawyers, legislators and other writers on behalf of her causes.

Thackeray's friendship and fascination with Caroline Norton began at least as early as 1832 and lasted at least as late as 1862. Their surviving correspondence is not extensive, but they were frequently in each other's company; Thackeray read her writings; and he wrote her story and her causes into his own writings – notably in three works. Caroline Norton's own story and, even more, her specific causes are written into *Barry Lyndon* in the person of Lady Lyndon who is abused by Barry and whose children are used by the violent husband as pawns in his battle to control his wife's property. Like the Norton story, Barry sends the children away to Scotland, out of reach of English custody laws, where, as happened to one of Caroline's sons, the Lyndon boy is killed in a fall from a horse. *Barry Lyndon* is an indictment of English law, which allows men to abuse women with impunity, and a vindication of the life and causes of Caroline Norton. It is not likely that many original readers of the novel could have missed the broad implications of Thackeray's indictment of the law, even if, perhaps, they missed the pointed parallels between Thackeray's story of the Lyndons and the one played out in the newspapers about the Nortons.

Perhaps more pointed are the parallels between Caroline Norton and Becky Sharp in *Vanity Fair*, who, admittedly, differs from Norton first in having no heart and secondly in having a husband, Rawdon, who though somewhat rough cut is worth loving. But, in wit,

*Figure 6.4* Vignette for ch. 44, of Becky as siren, *Vanity Fair*, 439

beauty, 'famous frontal development', business sense, poise, manipulation and declarations of innocence, there is an uncanny likeness between Becky and Caroline. For Thackeray it could not have been more clear that the lovely, helpless, vulnerable, dependent Amelia, so like his own now hopelessly mad wife Isabella, was being judged in comparison to a beautiful, independent, strong, intelligent counter in the person of Becky. Amelia, he remarked in a letter of July 1848, was 'always an overrated woman I thought'.[75] But, his fascination with and admiration for Caroline Norton seems never to have gone beyond friendship, for Thackeray's appreciation for the 'milk and water' women of his life left him, it seems, also a bit wary of the stronger variety, about whom he was never sure if 'it was all just talk' or if there were unsavory matters swirling in the murky depths below the surface, as he suggested about the siren Becky. It happens that in 1848, as *Vanity Fair* was coming to a conclusion, the battle between George and Caroline Norton was again heating up in the press, this time over property rights. So, again, it is very likely that original readers recognized a parallel between Becky's and Caroline's life and marital problems.

But the aspect of the Norton marriage relationship that most touched Thackeray was the way in which the law supported the abuses by men of their unprotected wives. And the work in which

*Figure 6.5* Steel engraved plate of Becky's first appearance as Clytemnestra, *Vanity Fair*, 512

Thackeray deals most effectively and directly with this issue in the lives of ordinary upper-middle-class citizens is in *The Newcomes*, where Caroline Norton reappears in the person of Clara Newcome, who also signs her letters C.N. Barnes Newcome is a hated scoundrel whose knowledge of British law is sufficient to enable him to use it to the fullest in prosecuting Clara. Never mind that Barnes had an illegitimate family, discarded at his marriage, or that he is unfaithful to Clara whom he abuses verbally, physically, emotionally, and economically, rendering her an emotional basket case; for the law is on his side, and Clara's escape from Barnes, when she runs away with the rough looking but gentle Jack Belsize, costs her her reputation, her wealth, and, most cruel of all, her children. Thackeray enlists all of the reader's sympathy on the side of the suffering woman, though he portrays clearly enough both the righteous triumph of the tyrannical husband and the moral indignation of conventional onlookers who judge the principals by what they think should be the case rather than by the facts of the case. The Newcome story recalls doggerel verse Thackeray had written five years earlier which concludes:

> Though you promised to protect her, though you promised to defend her;
> You are welcome to neglect her: to the devil you may send her;
> You may strike her, curse, abuse her; so declares our law renowned
> And if after this you lose her, – why, you're paid two hundred pound.

Barnes wins his crim. con. case against Jack Belsize and is awarded damages. Though it is seldom recorded in critical assessments of *The Newcomes*, its original publication was certainly a central and effective instrument in the passage of the Marital Causes Act of 1857.[76]

In addition to these important relationships with women, Thackeray developed with many other women social friendships that apparently thrived on his charming, gallant, but utterly safe status as a 'single man' who was married. The condition lent piquancy and restraint to relationships that supplied his genuine need for and interest in feminine companionship. Among male Victorian novelists, Thackeray stands alone in the estimation of modern feminist critics for his understanding of women's issues, for standing up for the rights of women, and for standing against their legal victimization by husbands and fathers. Feminists have delighted in reading against the grain of Victorian gender–culture conventions and finding Thackeray to be subtly in harmony with their criticism of those conventions.[77]

After the derangement of his wife in 1840, there is a sensitivity to women and their forced role of inferiority, particularly noticeable in *The Great Hoggarty Diamond* (1841) but visible in *Barry Lyndon* (1844) and other more clearly satiric works, that suggests a side of Thackeray and his work that is special. In *The Great Hoggarty Diamond* it is shown that 'the best diamond a man can wear in his bosom is the love of a wife and children', by which it seems clear that a good woman is better than luck or money because she will make honest subsistence possible. However, many readers seem to think that it means that the manly, satiric side of Thackeray, evident in works like *Yellowplush* (1837) and *Gahagan* (1839) in which there is a sneaking admiration for tough macho men, is tamed by sentiment. And since sentiment never has the power to move that is associated with passion, awe, and fear, critics have tended to neglect *The Great Hoggarty Diamond* and to account for it as the product of remorse and chastening brought to Thackeray by the loss of his wife and by his sense of guilt for neglecting her. But Sam Titmarsh's wife, Mary, is no Isabella Shaw. Sam is a fool, no doubt, and his naive trust and delight in a succession of lucky and improbable investments is both endearing and repelling, for we can see disaster coming long before it strikes. Sam, who holds conventional notions that women are not fit for the world of men and belong by nature in domestic conditions where they require protection, tries his best to shield his Mary, whom he always describes as being in a delicate condition. But in the end it is Mary's strength, intelligence and resourcefulness that rescues the family and restores Sam to a condition in which he can provide barely 51 per cent of the support for his family, the rest coming from Mary's annuity.

It is true that the overt 'moral' of this novelette is that high risk and high gains are a devil's game and that hard work and a mere 4 per cent on investments is bound to win in the end. Memory of Thackeray's own addiction to gambling and his gambling losses might cause us to think this is another attempt to write what conscience, not appetite, dictates. But it is Thackeray's depiction of a man's dependence upon women that provides the basic beat in this story.

The main point here is that by 1841 and the writing of *The Great Hoggarty Diamond*, Thackeray exhibits an ability to expose the pride and weakness of conventional men and to acknowledge the strength and intelligence of women. It is this domestic 'knowledge' and sensitivity to women and their position in society that become a major issue in the later fiction. Unable to know a good woman when they see her and attached to a stereotypical ideal for women, men of ordinary stupidity are exposed devastatingly in the portrait of Colonel Newcome, who pines his life away in regret over Madame d'Ivry, yet force feeds Rosey MacKenzie to Clive, who would rather have Ethel and who, not untypical of his gender, makes nearly all the mistakes known to man about women. Perhaps this puts the case too harshly, for generations of readers have shared Pendennis's approval of Clive because he is good looking and of his father because he is soft hearted, and many have thought, sentimentally, that in *The Newcomes* Thackeray had finally written a 'good book' – one in which good people were not gullible fools.

Nevertheless, if Clive does not like his poor wife, Rosey, why does he impregnate her five times, producing four out of five babies stillborn and, in effect, killing Rosey in her final confinement? This is a troubling question about Thackeray's attitudes toward women and toward his fiction. It seems highly probable that the book's approval of Colonel Newcome and of Clive is to be laid at the feet of its narrator, Arthur Pendennis, rather than at the feet of the author, Thackeray. It is Pendennis who approves of Colonel Newcome for his gallant romantic but stupid acts with regard to every woman in his life save his mother and foster mother. And it is Pendennis who approves of Clive for his good looks and good intentions, Pendennis who joins in Clive's anti-intellectual attitudes toward art, and Pendennis who thinks nothing unusual of Clive's unconscionable treatment of Rosey, first in marrying her when he did not love her and then in keeping her both pregnant and at arm's length. The approval of these two men in *The Newcomes* reflects the weaknesses of Arthur Pendennis as we have come to know him in *The History of Pendennis* where a worldly uncle, a narrow-minded mother, and a sweet prig of a sister/cousin/wife save Pendennis in a series of brushes with the social and domestic disasters into which his own social conditioning led him naturally.

To arrive at this fine distinction between author and narrator requires the correlation of three major strands in Thackeray's life: first, his love life and relationships with women; secondly, his religious and philosophical ideas regarding how mankind knows what it thinks it knows and therefore what a narrator can know; and finally his financial condition and role as a professional author. When these strands are understood in relation to each other, it becomes clear that Arthur Pendennis ran interference for his author by posing as a conventional, publicly approved voice uttering in approbation positions that the author, Thackeray, undercut but did not expose so obviously as to alienate the conventional Victorian reader and book purchaser. It is worth noting that, while critical objections to Thackeray's later works have been voiced over and over in the 150 years since the success of *Vanity Fair* supposedly spoiled him as an author and compromised his art, the fact is that during his life, each new novel sold more or made more money than its predecessor for Thackeray and, with the exception of *The Virginians*, made more money for his publisher as well. From a financial point of view, from the conventional view of Thackeray's readers, he made all the right moves. A fuller understanding of his philosophy, morality and narrative technique may show that they were the right artistic moves as well.

But he did not make these moves unambiguously or unironically. Thackeray learned profound lessons about uncertainty, about women, about men (himself included), and about duplicity and betrayals that made him sensitive above the norm to every person's susceptibility to self-deception. These insights form the foundation of his characterizations and his plot developments. At the same time, he was a professional author, dependent on his quill for sustenance, and he had no intention of killing the goose that laid his nest eggs – alienating the paying public – by a desire to preachify and save the world from its follies.

In brief, the three strands of Thackeray's life, thought, and circumstances that come together to support a clear distinction between his own and Pendennis's views are: That in his relationships with women he knew enough about his wife, his cousin, his two 'lovers', and his famous acquaintance Caroline Norton, to know that Colonel Newcome and Clive know next to nothing about women and could not be admired for their treatment of them. Pendennis's admiration for them is conventional and based in his far more limited understanding of women than Thackeray's. Pendennis's approval of Clive and the Colonel cannot be Thackeray's. Thackeray's philosophical conviction that uncertainty dogs every aspect of human knowledge committed him to taking positions tentatively and to exercising a tolerance which sought first to extend understanding rather than condemnation to the world's 'sinners', including those whose sin consisted of being so virtuous that they did harm. Finally, as a writer who had to earn his living by his writing, rather than an ideologue who would or could offend for principle's sake, he was bound to sugarcoat and veil his position, revealing it with kid gloves rather than risking the alienation of the paying public upon whom he depended. In the end, he probably reached more people who were made to ponder their own positions by the tact that he chose than he would have had he been blunter in his attack on what he considered the ordinary and generally acceptable domestic cruelties of contemporary life.

# 7
# Thackeray's Men

Thackeray drew the majority of his characters from the middle ranks of life. In *Vanity Fair*, however, he toyed with the idea of writing a Newgate novel of low life or a Silverfork novel of high life, rejecting both because he had never been to prison and had no entrée to the homes of the aristocracy. Yet, the range of male characters in his fiction is exceedingly large. Their portraits expose both the individual foibles of the three-dimensional characters that they are and the conventional models of male conduct forming the images of men at the time.

These two concepts are worth trying to flesh out. Thackeray seldom constructs characters as stereotypes. He has, of course, a bevy of characters named John, James, Jeames or Jack who are, almost always, tall footmen, and he has other characters named Rincer, Blenkinsop or Flanagan, or Molly, Polly, Mary or Martha who just as frequently are serving women. And as long as these characters remain in their official roles, they are undifferentiated wooden models, though the serving women can bend at the waist to peer or listen through keyholes. But the moment such characters step into the narrative they become James Morgan, the capitalist, or Jeames Yellowplush, the literary hack, or Miss Horrocks, the pliable mistress, or Mrs Lightfoot, formerly Mrs Bonner, who knows her mistress so well she can speak for her *in absentia*. And each has character flaws, social ineptitudes and ideological quirks that come into narrative play. None is a decoration, mere prop, or the butt of an off-hand joke. (Perhaps the closest thing to an exception is Hodson, a street boy who became a barber in Clavering and who moonlights as a waiter at a dinner given by Pen while he was canvassing for votes as a prospective Member of Parliament in Sir Francis Clavering's place. Hodson is the butt of two jokes on his trade as barber: he drops a plate because his 'hands are slippery with bear's grease' [hair ointment] and as mere waiter he serves hare and partridge, prompting Arthur to suggest that he should have '*cut the Hare*'. Having served his purpose, so to speak, Hodson is never seen again.)

Of course, Thackeray's major characters are even more complexly developed. Far from serving as illustrations of a single characteristic, they harbor contradictions and inconsistencies common to our own acquaintances. The good Helen Pendennis nurses a life-long secret passion for her first love, Francis Bell, though she adequately and conventionally worships her husband John. She believes young Arthur a paragon and, yet, at the first whiff of suspicion assumes that he is guilty of base intrigue and whoredom. She loves and nurtures Laura as a daughter, but in a fit of anger blames *her* for Arthur's supposed sins. Helen abandons her plans for a marriage between Laura and Arthur when she believes Arthur has committed himself with Fanny Bolton, but she grieves as if she had lost her own lover. And Thackeray repeatedly notes the ways in which mother love and erotic love are confused, both by young men and older women – witness the May–September union in *Pendennis* of young Frederick Lightfoot and the matronly Mrs Bonner who 'regarded that youth with a fondness at once parental and conjugal'.

But just as important as noting the individuality, complexity and richness of the character portrayals, the second point is that Thackeray's characters are seldom eccentrics. They are ordinary, common, conventional, identifiable members of any Victorian community. Unlike Dickens's characters, who for all their range of recognizable commonness each seems to have a unique exaggerated gesture or habit, Thackeray's characters remain outwardly realistic, whatever oddities might motivate their behavior. Thackeray's circle of acquaintance was very wide within the allegedly narrow confines of the upper middle classes. It included men and women in many trades from publishing, shopkeeping, millinery, haberdashery and bill discounters to jewelers, bankers, stockbrokers and shippers; he knew gamblers, theatre personalities, singers, dancers, military youths and retirees, East India men and women, saddlers, hostlers and cabmen; he knew a whole range of dinner- and party-giving aristocrats and would-be aristocrats, clergymen, lawyers and medical men. But more important, I believe, is the fact that Thackeray had thought deeply about the conventions that make men men and women women. Social rank had its forming effects, yes, but expectations about male behavior and female behavior crossed social classes. Men were, conventionally, the masters. No number of individual cases in which men were hen-pecked or dominated by their women changed the fact that the convention was that men were masters. Similarly, boys were their mother's delights. No number of cases to the contrary changed the fact that mothers dote on sons (or should). Women, regardless of individual cases, were retiring, demure, submissive and dependent. Independent women were always exceptions; they may abound but they were contrary to convention.

The importance of this notion that individual character development takes place in an atmosphere of conventional standards for behavior is at least two-fold: First, every depiction of individual behavior is monitored against an unspoken but conventional notion of behavior that everyone is privy to – writer, readers and the cast of characters in the fiction; it is unspoken because it is generally known and for that reason is also not written in the text, though readers in our day may no longer be in the know. Secondly, whenever a character develops according to convention, it goes without saying that conventional people approve of the character. Thus Laura Bell (in *Pendennis*), Amelia Sedley (in *Vanity Fair*) and Caroline Gann (in *A Shabby Genteel Story*) pass our scrutiny with barely a second look. They are not only approved characters, they are uninteresting characters. So, when Thackeray lards his narrative with questions about their goodness or shows the ways in which these good characters are cruel or selfish, the conventional reader assumes that Thackeray is inept. The conventional eye follows, instead, Becky Sharp (in *Vanity Fair*), Blanche Amory (in *Pendennis*), Beatrix Esmond (in *Esmond*) and (very disturbingly) Ethel Newcome (in *The Newcomes*) because they provide constant and unpredictable interruptions to conventional development for women. They are not unusual women. Readers from Thackeray's time to the present can name a woman of their ilk from the circle of their own acquaintance, but they violate the tacit conventions for good women, and the conventional eye sees in them the behavior that is to be labeled bad. When *un*conventional women are good, such readers suspect them of duplicity; when the conventional women are bad, such readers suspect Thackeray of inattention. Readers who credit Thackeray with control over his work might instead think that he is counting on readers to expect realistic and insightful portrayals of individual characters who, like people in real life, combine conventional with unconventional behavior and do not always speak their lines from the play book. Clichés do not account for their behavior.

To develop this idea of Thackeray's use of conventions for male and female behavior, we can do worse than follow 12 men portrayed in *The History of Pendennis*. Though Thackeray seems not to have emphasized their pairing, they can conveniently be introduced that way here. The two nearly unmitigated scoundrels are Sir Francis Clavering and Colonel Altamont (alias Armstrong and Amory); both are married to Miss Snell that was, the extremely wealthy daughter of a reprobate India entrepreneur. (To be fair, both Clavering and his bride thought she was a widow when they married.) Both men are predators, using and abusing the naive and good natured lady in all the ways sanctioned by law and in some ways that were illegal besides.

James Morgan and Captain Strong form an uncomfortable pair, who for much of the book appear to be the servants and appendages of Major Pendennis and Francis Clavering, respectively. Both are stealthy or secretive, neither is well-known by his master, but both turn on their masters in the end: Morgan in an attempt to out-blackmail the blackmailing Major, and Strong in an attempt to prevent further abuse of his Lady by Sir Francis. Thackeray takes the time their masters did not bother to give in order to understand their motivations: Morgan's sycophantic social and financial aspirations and willingness to deceive and cheat to gain his ends, and Strong's self-confidence, independence and willingness to sacrifice himself for the good of others.

Major Pendennis and Captain Costigan, former warriors and ostensible guardians of the best interests of the younger generation, form another uneasy couple, for Costigan, whose military history may be a fiction, swaggers and talks very big but acts very small while Major Pendennis, an old campaigner, speaks little, believes less, and maneuvers strategically within an inch of a great victory – which he later declares himself lucky to have lost. Costigan comes very close to being a caricature, the feckless Irish drunk. But even here Thackeray takes time to rescue the old man, sending young Huxter like a good Samaritan to nurse him as a victim of forces greater than himself. The Major, too, skates near to caricature, the pompous returned East India man. But he is a man of the world with a range of acquaintances and experiences and the cunning, when finally awakened to the doings of his valet Morgan, to best him at his own game, even as he had met Costigan in the early chapters and won the field in a bloodless display of verbal skill and knowledge of human nature. Both men remain, however, locked in essentially male and unselfconscious roles available to conventional Victorian men.

Mr Henry Foker, Esq., heir to wealthy brewers' vats, forms, with Mr Bows the theatrical coach and organist, another unequal pair. Both play waiting games for women who choose other men, both pass advice as if their experience of the world rendered them immune to the maladies that, nevertheless, ruin their hopes for bliss with a woman. Bows devotes himself in a forlorn way, first to Emily Fotheringay and then to Fanny Bolton, and ends being used and discarded by each one. His reaction is a bitterness that causes him to say things that are not true but which taint Fanny's reputation. Foker, similarly, devotes himself to Blanche, but unlike the case of the penniless Bows, the woman plays for Foker and nearly lands him before her duplicity, machinations and betrayals are revealed in the nick of time to save him from her. Foker's reaction is, perhaps, less bitter than Bows', but there seems no shadow of potential marital disaster in his future at the end of the book.

Sam Huxter and the Revd. Mr Smirke also occupy similar roles. Both aspire to rank or images of rank that lie out of their reach, both are bold in their cups and timid and weak in the breach of any crisis, each marries a woman who is stronger than he. And both serve as conventional standards against which Arthur Pendennis's measure is taken. Sam, who like Pen is an apothecary's son, wins and wears Fanny with whom Pen had dallied. Thackeray goes to great lengths to assert Pen's innocence, but it is an innocence akin to Becky Sharp's with Lord Steyne. Perhaps no sexual encounter occurred, but the thought of it was clearly present; and the act may have been avoided by accident rather than intent. Such episodes are probably what Thackeray had in mind when he noted in the Preface to the *History of Pendennis* that 'Since the author of Tom Jones was buried, no writer of fiction among us has been permitted to depict to his utmost power a Man. We must drape him, and give him a conventional simper.' Tom Jones, of course, had a variety of sexual encounters not permitted to Pen. In short, Sam Huxter does the right thing at some risk to himself: he risks his father's wrath to marry Fanny. Pen, on the other hand, serves himself, not Fanny, by escaping temptation and doing 'the right thing' by not having to marry Fanny. Smirke's longing love for Helen Pendennis is at least as pure and careful as any love affair in the book. He is Pen's hired intellectual and spiritual leader (a description that makes me laugh every time I think of it), but Smirke consoles himself with a girl from Clapham provided by his evangelical mother, and after her death he sets up a high-Anglican chapel in Tunbridge Wells where he is patronized by Blanche Amory who briefly finds religion a useful toy.

Finally, we come to Arthur Pendennis and George Warrington. In conversation with Charlotte Brontë one evening at the home of their publisher, George Smith, Thackeray referred to himself as Pendennis, to which Miss Brontë immediately said, 'No, George Warrington, you mean.' Both were right and both were wrong. Thackeray had the physique, taste for tobacco, experience living alone and the newspaper practice of George Warrington. More important, he had the marital history and consequent forlorn love life of George. When George recounts how he fell in love and made promises he had to keep and, so, married a woman totally inappropriate for him, from whom he separated, but for whom he continued to be financially responsible, Thackeray combined his own story of a wild liaison with an older woman of a lower class and his actual marriage to a woman he could not live with. But what probably prompted Miss Brontë most was George's seriousness and unambiguous moral rectitude, which she had conceived as Thackeray's underlying character from her reading of *Vanity Fair*. However, only the pattern is similar: George is a great, hulking, intelligent, trapped man who falls forlornly in love with a girl he cannot have because he was married already. Thackeray was a great, hulking, intelligent man trapped in marriage that, love match though it was, had failed, and he was forlornly in love with his best friend's wife. George belongs to his estranged wife, and Laura 'belongs' to Pen as much as Jane Octavia Brookfield belonged to the Revd. William Brookfield. George's tender and discreet longing for Laura is very like Thackeray's arm's length desire for Jane.

The differences between Thackeray and his character as Warrington are as glaring as the similarities, of course, for *The History of Pendennis* is not a thinly veiled autobiography or an unimaginative incorporation of actual events. George is a political writer whose understanding of economics, legislation, and world affairs exceeds Thackeray's. It is true that Thackeray wrote political journalism for *The Morning Chronicle*, that he wrote a long, two-piece essay on Louis-Philippe for *The Westminster Review* in a bid to become that journal's editor, but his forte was the light, humorous, social satire of *Punch* and *Fraser's Magazine*. And Warrington's highly moral and conventional reaction to Arthur's moral dilemmas (the Fanny Bolton affair, the Blanche Amory affair, the seat in Parliament, Pen's accusation of his Mother for tampering with his mail) is so conventional and so pious that it is impossible to see Thackeray in those Warrington speeches. Charlotte Brontë was the more ready to see Thackeray as Warrington because, having early declared him to be the social regenerator of the age on the basis of her reading of *Vanity Fair*, she much preferred Thackeray in the role of Warrington to that of Pendennis. The fictional Lady Rockminster's similar preference for Warrington echoes the sentiment.

In significant ways and in spite of his facetious claim, Thackeray was also unlike Arthur. His early love passages did not end in marriage to an older incompatible woman, as did George's, but neither did he escape his Fanny Bolton, who for him was Isabella Shawe, whom he loved dearly and to whom he believed he was doing his duty, but realized the match was a mistake long before she became deranged and had to be institutionalized. Also unlike Pendennis, Thackeray never found Laura. Nevertheless, in the end, I think, Thackeray had more of an emotional and intellectual affinity with Pendennis, as he is portrayed in *Pendennis* than with Warrington, though I shall soon return to what I think are the crucial differences between writer and character. Above all, Arthur Pendennis is an ordinary English lad. He was 'no better than he should be,' though his mother generally thought him a paragon. He was no scholar, though poetry and language came to him easily. He lacked application and discipline, though he was capable of extraordinary exertion in pursuit of his desires. He was destined for a career, a social rank, and a marital status that virtually went without saying, though everyone knew it was the 'dear widow's greatest wish' that he fulfill her dreams and marry Laura. All preparations were made to insure his success: his father started his college fund, his mother hired a tutor, his uncle monitored his introduction to college, and little Laura, waiting in the wings, urged him to make a name for himself. The rest is an ordinary downhill history of small failures and even smaller successes until, having done all the things that all the other ordinary boys of his age did at college, he fails his exams and comes home in debt and disgrace. But his shame is not of the character-molding type. He is still the prince of Fairoaks, a superior being for whom his mother and his Laura labor and sacrifice to support. Pen takes these women as his due because he is an ordinary man for whom it is ordinary for women to suffer and sacrifice. Pen is the product of the conventional notion that man is master.

Thackeray is not the first writer to choose as his principal character a person with repelling characteristics. One of the most influential critical books of the 20th-century, Wayne Booth's *The Rhetoric of Fiction*, explains how Jane Austen manages to salvage the reader's toleration of Emma long enough for Emma to undergo the lessons and personality changes necessary to make that priggish busybody attractive enough to be a suitable mate to Mr Knightly. One is tempted to assume that Thackeray has a similar problem holding the reader's condemnation of Arthur Pendennis at bay long enough for that self-satisfied, arrogant, impetuous, selfish, insensitive, artificial, womanizing snob to learn the lessons necessary before he can be given to Laura without a reader revolt. Several strategies apparent in the narrative might support this view. The narrator is constantly berating Pen as a selfish young naive person, thus saving the reader the trouble of condemning him. At the same time the narrator focuses attention on the few good qualities the boy exhibits, showing how his honest intentions, his openness, and his abhorrence of overt lies mitigate somewhat his propensity to self-deception and self-indulgence. And we are given frequent hints that time and tribulation will teach Arthur the lessons he needs. For readers with some knowledge of Thackeray's own life, particularly as narrated by Gordon Ray in his first volume, titled *The Uses of Adversity*, it is not difficult to imagine in Pendennis's education a version of Thackeray's own lessons learned.

Several aspects of this narrative, however, mitigate against this hopeful view. The first is, that while the title of the book and the

*Figure 7.1* Vignette for ch. 26, in which Pendennis renews acquaintance with Blanche Amory, *Pendennis*, II, 257

narrative line focus on Pendennis, the emphasis seems always to lie with the women. Readers learn far more about women than Pendennis ever learns. He never realizes the extent to which Emily Fotheringay, Fanny Bolton, and even Blanche Amory, but especially Laura Bell are vulnerable dependents. There is no reason that Pendennis should ever learn that. The women of the novel exist in a conventional world where they are by nature dependent. Their vulnerability is an aspect of male protectiveness. From Pen's point of view a real woman is one that can benefit from his protective nature. From his point of view, his honorable actions save Fanny Bolton (as well as himself) from social disaster. But Thackeray's text is full of very explicit descriptions of female vulnerability. We can begin with the very last words of the book, found in the Preface, written after the book was completed. In the words already quoted the writer laments that it has been impossible to portray a young man like Pendennis as he really is. Even Helen Pendennis would know how to understand that line. She assumes Arthur had seduced and had sex with Fanny; Major Pendennis assumes it; Laura assumes it; Warrington assumes it; Sam Huxter assumes it on the night Pen walks in Vauxhall Gardens with Fanny on his arm when he first met her. In Victorian novels some things had to go without saying and so it seems in *Pendennis*: a man in good clean linen with a white top hat goes by himself to Vauxhall Gardens on a Friday night to pick up a certain kind of woman and ... and the rest goes without saying because as Laura points out, it is not fitting for such things to be spoken of before her.

So, everybody knows what Pen has been up to and each has his or her own take on it and on what Pen should now do. The Major wants him to forget Fanny because according to male conventions she was nothing but a Vauxhall fling. Pen's Mother wants him to make them both honest by marrying her, since by women's conventions it is the honorable thing to do. Laura wants to feel moral indignation against Pen and make him do what his Mother says no matter what. Only there is a minor problem: Pen ain't guilty. But he has a hard time getting anybody to believe him. And he is not guilty in the same way Becky is not guilty of sleeping with Lord Steyne – something intervened before the fact that would have been. And what Arthur 'learned' was that he had escaped an episode that could have ruined his chances in life because from his point of view women are the seductresses and ever since Eve have led men into perdition. Men, in that view, are the weak, vulnerable victims of the wiles of women.

Even Pen's mother believes that. By her lights, Arthur must marry Fanny if Fanny succeeded in seducing him. And, the mother's goofy logic goes on, if it isn't Fanny's fault for seducing him, then it is Laura's fault for not marrying him and saving him from temptation. When will it be Arthur's fault? Never, by his mother's account.

Of course, in the end Arthur does marry Laura. The Good Laura is the reward given to the reformed, repentant prince of Fairoaks, who in my opinion has learned almost nothing that Thackeray, I believe, had learned through adversity. Thackeray learned that it was not Isabella's fault he had fallen in love with her and married her. It was not her fault that he neglected her and left her with house and children to keep – tasks for which she was clearly inadequate – while he pursued the Muse and the necessary shillings to keep food on the table. Thackeray learned the pain and unfairness of what most Victorians took for the natural order: that women, married and unmarried, were vulnerable dependents. Thackeray shows that he knows there is something wrong with this concept of 'nature' by the innumerable instances in *The History of Pendennis* where he details the woes of women. Mrs Fribsby runs off to France and comes back betrayed by a worthless husband; Mrs Bonner consoles herself with the young Lightfoot whose last sober moment predated the nuptials; Miss Snell marries the sailor Amory who has his court appointed reasons to disappear and pretend to die, but who comes back to haunt her life and resume the hunt for her fortune; Sir Francis, also hunting her fortune, weds her and hates her. And all these patterns of behavior are perfectly understandable, for the laws of England upheld them. In spite of the fact that Miss Snell, that is Lady Clavering, that is, Mrs Amory, was still married to Amory, who was only thought to be dead when she married Sir Francis Clavering, Sir Francis's son Frank, who strictly speaking is illegitimate, will inherit the Snell fortune, not Betsy 'Blanche' Amory the only truly legitimate child, because – because Frank is male. No other reason is necessary. It goes without saying.

That Pendennis did not learn the lessons that seem so obvious to readers of his story becomes abundantly clear when he takes over the job of narrating Thackeray's later novels. Skipping, for the moment, Thackeray's next novel, *The History of Henry Esmond*, because it is narrated by the eponymous hero, we take up *The Newcomes* where Pendennis's perspective invades every line until the famous literal line drawn across the page in the last installment when Thackeray takes the pen away from Pen to inscribe the final paragraphs.

Thackeray remarked that he was more comfortable writing *The Newcomes* and we can suppose also *The Virginians*, and *Philip*, with Arthur Pendennis posing as the author. He wrote to Sarah Baxter about *The Newcomes*, 'I am not to be the author of it. Mr Pendennis is to be the writer of his friend's memoirs and by the help of this little mask (wh. I borrowed from Pisistratus Bulwer I suppose) shall be able to talk more at ease than in my own person. I only thought of the plan last night and am immensely relieved by adopting it.'[78]

It has never been clear to anyone commenting on it exactly how this strategy gave Thackeray comfort, relief, or ease in expressing himself. For a long time I assumed that a writer would choose a persona to speak who could more freely express opinions that might seem radical or controversial. Pendennis seems, in some ways, the sort of character who had learned his lessons in the novel that bears his name and therefore could serve as a buffer between Thackeray and his audience through whom Thackeray could say his mind and yet appear to be expressing only the opinions of his characters. I no longer think that is the most likely explanation.

Another possibility is that Pendennis is simply a first person narrator who reveals as much about himself as about the characters whom he describes and on whom he comments. Certainly Thackeray had done that sort of thing before. Barry Lyndon, speaking in his own voice, says many things and adopts many tones that few have attributed to Thackeray or that he would have wanted attributed to him. The differences between Thackeray and Barry have seemed obvious to all 20th-century commentators on that novel except film-maker Stanley Kubrick, who made a sympathetic character of Barry in the film, thus fulfilling Barry's best hope to have conned yet another naive reader into thinking he was a fine fellow. Another notable difference between Lyndon and Pendennis as narrators is that the purpose for the Lyndon disguise seems not unlike that underlying many of Robert Browning's dramatic monologues: to call the reader's imaginative, analytical and moral skills to bear on the reading so that reader and author enjoy an alliance against the speaker's judgments and values. The narrator stands, thus, exposed by his own lack of self-awareness.

In *Pendennis*, as we have noted, we find not an unself-conscious rogue or villain, but an ordinary Englishman not unlike the run of his peers, with doting mothers and adoring wives, but whose private lives were best not examined too closely. In *The Newcomes* it is not hard to see the narrator presenting himself as an ordinary man whose sins are bland and conventional and whose insensitivities are common and usually overlooked by the other characters. Since Pen is the narrator, however, the author has no chance to insert commentary on him. So, if Thackeray was treating Pendennis as a first person narrator who could be exposed by his own words and judgments, there was an even greater risk than he ran with Lyndon that readers would think they were meant to agree with Pendennis, not that they were meant to be critical of his judgment and character.

Nevertheless, readers of *The Newcomes*, narrated by Pendennis, might frequently be offended by his approval of Colonel Newcome, whose matchmaking seems ultimately as cruel, self-seeking and misguided as Lady Kew's. And Pen's approval of Clive frequently borders on the maudlin and occasionally leaves something to be desired, as was suggested by the observation, in the previous chapter, that Clive dislikes his wife but keeps her pregnant. Reflection suggests that it was a mistake to think that the source of Thackeray's relief deciding upon Pendennis as narrator derived from a resulting freedom to be more perspicuous, more precise, in criticizing social norms. Rather, it now appears, Pendennis is being set up just as Lyndon was to expose the weaknesses and insensitivities of a speaker, but unlike Lyndon, the differences between the speaker's and the ordinary reader's points of view are not so obvious. Readers who fail to see that Pendennis should be criticized fall, by their mistake, into believing that Thackeray, through Pendennis, is approving of that which many ordinary Victorian readers found perfectly normal: men as masters, women as subservient, a double standard of morality, lack of concern for the plight of the poor, and other ordinary beliefs of the middle class.

It seems rather obvious now that Thackeray's insights into ordinary insensitivities, legal crimes (against women and children in particular), socially acceptable cruelties and egoisms had a tendency of hitting home too closely and perhaps, therefore, of damaging sales. For example, in the first edition of *Pendennis*, Thackeray describes Helen Thistlewood as one who 'suffered under such an infernal tyranny as only women can inflict on, or bear from, one another'.[79] This passage was omitted in the revised edition as were many other somewhat cutting remarks about common ordinary cruelties. It seems reasonable to think that, true though such observations are, they did not tend to increase Thackeray's popularity. And so, for the sake of his own image and of sales, the limits of his attack on 'legal crimes' was drawn back a bit. That of course is mere speculation. But it does stand to reason that it is more popular to attack the sins of the wicked than to expose the hypocrisies of the respectable.

But the possibility of using a narrative technique in which the realization of evil must be inferred by the reader rather than spelled out in straightforward authorial commentary became doubly evident to me when a student once looked up suddenly during a discussion of Henry Esmond as narrator of his own memoirs to say: 'Well, Esmond is just like Barry Lyndon, only genteel. He is just as insensitive and egoistical, but all within socially acceptable norms. No wonder Thackeray put his story into Esmond's own words.' This too is speculation, but it lends support to the notion that Thackeray's comfort in 'hiding behind' Arthur Pendennis as narrator of *The Newcomes* derived from the fact that Pendennis could show himself to be insensitive in socially acceptable ways: he could be appreciative of Clive, who, though he does not much like his wife and though she finds childbirth difficult, keeps her pregnant till she dies – for which Pen as narrator never blames Clive. It is difficult to believe that Thackeray didn't see it that way in a book so obviously about the uses and abuses of women.

Whereas in *The Luck of Barry Lyndon* reader and author agree against the narrator, in *The Newcomes* the reader is constantly invited to agree with a narrator who may seem like the author's alterego – except that to do so puts one too frequently into complicity with legal crimes and socially acceptable cruelties. It is easy enough for Thackeray or Pendennis to show how evil Barnes Newcome and Lady Kew and Madame d'Ivry are, but not so easy to show the equally cruel consequences of conventionally good characters like Clive, the Colonel and Ethel. It seems possible that Thackeray chose Pendennis as a charming but frequently blind storyteller in order to mask his revelations that conventional, acceptable, ordinary, often well-intentioned persons perform their 'little' evils and pass unremarked much of the time.

Eve Kosofsky Sedgwick remarks parenthetically, in an essay on another subject, '(Of course, Thackeray's own ambiguous marital status – married, but to an inveterately sanitarium-bound, psychotically depressed woman – facilitated this slippage in the narrators whom Thackeray seemed to model on himself.)'. We could take this comment to mean that Pendennis was very like Thackeray at some previous more insensitive time of his life, leaving room for readers, whether knowledgeable about Thackeray's life or not, to have to work hard at the ethical questions raised by the story – occasionally approving and sometimes disapproving of the narrator's stance. It is easy to see the connections between the young Pendennis and the young Thackeray who had similar mothers and similar school experiences. But it is important to be able to dissociate narrator from author in *The Newcomes*, for that book raises too many questions about the uneven relationships of men and women about which we cannot agree with Pendennis. And we would quit in disgust and seriously underestimate the author, whom we know from his letters understood these problems, if we had to equate William Thackeray with Arthur Pendennis. Thackeray knew more than Arthur, even – or especially – when they were writing *The Newcomes*.

And yet it is Arthur who writes in *The Newcomes*: 'The wicked are wicked no doubt; and they go astray, and they fall, and they come by their deserts: but who can measure the mischief which the very virtuous do?' (I.184). The sentence suggests that Pendennis should know that his friendliest characters are capable of inflicting pain and even doing damage in the act of imposing their own notion of good upon others.

It is not odd that this chapter on Thackeray's men should end seeming to be so much about women, for though Thackeray knew the world of men – the law, the racetrack, the journalists' working dinners, and the dives and night haunts of men – he seems to define his men always in relationship to women. Lord Steyne whose power and wealth made it possible for him to use and disregard the services of women is judged primarily by his mistreatment of his wife and daughters-in-law. So is Old Osborne whose mantel clock celebrates Agamemnon's sacrifice of his daughter Iphigenia. William Dobbin is frequently identified as the only real gentleman in *Vanity Fair* and his entire life is devoted to a woman he and most readers agree in the end is not worth the sacrifice; nevertheless, Dobbin's selflessness puts him on a plane few of Thackeray's men ever achieve. Colonel Newcome, who occasionally rises to that level, as in his treatment of the woman who reared him, is faulted in the end because of his failure to understand the selfishness of his love for Rosey and judgmental stance he adopted toward Ethel.

# 8
# The Personal in the *Roundabout Papers*

Thackeray wrote the *Roundabout Papers* as regular editorial commentaries for the *Cornhill Magazine* from January 1860 to November 1863, the month before he died. From the first through the last, there are reminders that these are personal or familiar essays from Thackeray as editor of the *Cornhill* about editing the magazine or writing for it. Occasionally Thackeray addresses the readers of the *Cornhill*, warning potential writers of the protocols for submitting unsolicited manuscripts. But chief among the *Roundabout* themes are the pleasures of reading and discussing literature, the pleasures and annoyances of travel, a nostalgia for youth with its joys and follies, the importance and fragility of friendship, the relationships between servants and masters, the psychology of enmity, and expectations and disappointments in all areas of life. These themes show up in what could be characterized as familiar essays in the style of Charles Lamb: with quaint titles, loose structures, meandering from subject to subject until, in the end, the pieces all come together with a central chord plucked here and there performing a harmonium upon some point about youth or travel, children or follies, friendship or disappointment, etc. But from time to time the mode includes allegory as in 'Ogres' and 'On Two Roundabout Papers which I Intended to Write' or burlesque tales as in 'The Notch on the Axe', a spoof of sensational novels.

But I begin this roundabout approach to the *Roundabout Papers* with a look at the essays published from April to September 1861 because they strike me as extraordinarily revealing of a fundamental way Thackeray had of seeing his world, his society and himself. It is a commonplace in Thackeray criticism that he reflects notions of comedy he learned from the 18th-century novelist, Henry Fielding: that humor rises from two sources, neither of which requires distortion, exaggeration, or any sort of special treatment by the writer – only that he portray accurately what he sees. These two sources are vanity and hypocrisy. Vanity is the exaggeration of virtues actually possessed but greatly inflated by their possessor. Hypocrisy is the pretense to virtues not possessed except in sham. An accurate description of either reveals the real discrepancies between appearance and reality. In both cases there is a distance between appearance and reality, but it is created by the characters' distortions, not by the writer's exaggeration of reality.[80] It is certain that Thackeray was a brilliant student of his 18th-century master of comedy, but there is a profound difference between their visions of the world, a difference that propelled Fielding towards satire and Thackeray toward a humorous tolerance, for Fielding believed reality was observable and ascertainable, but Thackeray distrusted the observations he could not help but pursue. This difference may have been a reason for Charlotte Brontë to say that if Thackeray resembled Fielding he did so as an eagle resembles a vulture.[81] But it seems possible also that Fielding's more unbuttoned world may have contributed to that judgment as well.

At one level, 'On a Chalk-Mark on the Door' is an essay on the absurd commonplaces of social differences, and the pretensions of both masters and servants – commonplaces that provide routines of some comfort to both groups, but absurd on the face of it. 'We meet at every hour of the daylight, and are indebted to each other for a hundred offices of duty and comfort of life; and we live together for years, and don't know each other.'[82] The tragedies of servants' lives are routinely passed over or thought ludicrous; but, 'Lift these figures up but a story from the basement to the ground-floor, and the fun is gone. ... Why? Is it that the idea of persons at service is somehow ludicrous?' (181–2). One could read such an essay as the comments of a house owner pondering the deterioration of routines of comfort to the point of doubt about the propriety of asking his housemaid to do a better job cleaning the front door.

I believe this essay questions, fundamentally, the 'existence' of classes and rights and responsibilities. The basic order of English life, for masters and servants alike, class, rights, and responsibilities were set long ago and go without saying. Thackeray now comes forward to ask, why do they go without saying? For us, then, the question is, what or who was Thackeray that he should want to ask such a question. What aspect of his conscience was active in asking what justifies one's routine reliance on a convention in which our class of beings can demand of another class of beings that they look to and minister to our wants and needs while we utterly ignore theirs – except at pay day? Or to put it the other way, what justifies our routine acceptance of the responsibility to serve the needs of another class of people who do not care of fig for our welfare? Thackeray questions what goes without saying in his world so often that one comes to think of it as endemic to his character. He distrusts the routine, the ordinary comforts and established order even as he enjoys the fruits of such a society. Again our question is, why? Was he always so? What were the circumstances of his life and his imagination that led him to respond with the sensitivity this essay shows for points of view which he could under no circumstances have understood first hand?

A clue may be found in the next pair of essays, 'On Being Found Out' and 'On a Hundred Years Hence': the first about the terrors of being exposed for the rogue or fraud one is, and the second about the terrors and annoyances of being accused falsely and treated as one guilty of named and nameless sins uncommitted. Again, on one level, the first of these essays can be read as a simple exploration of the feelings of guilt when 'found out' or relief when not found out and of the usefulness of the daily escapes from detection that allow for civility and acceptance of fellow creatures in a world fraught with sufficient evil onto the day without having every foible exposed. And the second essay could, on the surface be read as a bitter reaction to any number of known and probably some unknown malicious stabs at, and tales about, Thackeray; for there were many of these, from the rumors about his supposed relationships with his daughters' governesses sparked by Charlotte Brontë's dedication to him of the second edition of *Jane Eyre*, through the series of attacks he endured from Irish readers detecting supposed, and perhaps some real, affronts to Irish pride in Thackeray's fiction, to the Garrick Club affair and the hurtful rumors about Thackeray being a mere front for the real editor of *The Cornhill*, George Smith its publisher.

In the light of the questions suggested by the previous essay, these two essays seem to me more fundamentally about the impossibility

*Figure 8.1* Self-portrait of the author begging mercy of Irish defenders of the honor of Miss Hayes. They had mistaken Thackeray's reference to a murderess (in *Catherine*) for a popular Irish singer of the same name, vignette for ch. 15, *Pendennis*, II, 139

of knowing one's self accurately and the necessity first to distrust what one knows about others. For the primary point of 'On Being Found Out' is that the driving curiosity of others to find you out is frequently mean and ugly, as in the opening anecdote about Mr Wiseacre trying to detect a petty thief by the ingenious device of making sleepy children stick their hands into a bag of soot. It is not only that Miserable Sinners need to be forgiven and let off; indeed, if M.S.'s are not let off, then the chaotic image of every M.S. being forever at the flogging post and no Jack Ketch to hang Jack Ketch (no hangman to hang the hangman) exposes absolute justice as a cartoon world *reductio ad absurdum*. We should be more concerned about knowing and acknowledging to ourselves our own weaknesses than to be trying to find out other folk. And, yet, from time to time we are found out, and we find out our neighbors because we give ourselves away as they do in their turn reveal themselves inadvertently by their acts. And the essay ends with an expression of relief that our women do not find us out, or, having found us out, do not give us away but protect us with an admirable hypocrisy of their own. But the final word is to the central rogue and hypocrite: 'You don't fancy you *are*, as you seem to them? No such thing, my man. Put away that monstrous conceit, and be thankful that *they* have not found you out' (199). As usual the moral is ambiguous, for it is hard to escape the feeling that one is being admonished to go on pretending one does not know that one's wife *has* found one out.

'On a Hundred Years Hence' is even more pointed in its exposure of falsehood, for it focuses not on pretensions but on gossip. Every story retold, whether by a new hearer or by the same person at some subsequent occasion, suffers the distortions of memory and misunderstanding and are embellished by the teller's desire to entertain or to shine by contrast. Truth, whatever it may be, has precious little to do with it. The two essays are tied together in the anecdote of the author's meeting with a woman who, to her surprise, discovers that he is not the monster she had been (mis)led to expect. 'I not only know that she had heard evil reports of me, but I know who told her – one of those acute fellows, my dear brethren, of whom we spoke in a previous sermon, who has found me out – found out actions which I never did, found out thoughts and sayings which I never spoke and judged me accordingly. Ah, my lad! have I found *you* out? *O risum teneatis*. Perhaps the person I am accusing is no more guilty than I' (211). The closing phrase is telling, for it is not gossip against which the essayist rails but against believing that one is right. Did he not, earlier in the essay have to confess that, having made 'some pathetic remarks about our propensity to believe ill of our neighbours' had caught himself out straightway believing a false story he heard about another friend? '*O mea culpa, mea maxima culpa*!' It is bad that we desire to think ill of one another, but it is worse that we believe such tales are true without bothering to check.

These essays, which Thackeray freely calls sermons, offer contrary tendencies as preferable: the tendency to overlook peccadilloes, not ferret them out and punish them; the tendency to doubt ill reports and to suppress them; and the tendency to recognize that the truth is often complex and uncertain. This is the same author who in *The Newcomes* remarked that 'the wicked ... would receive their just reward; but who can measure the mischief which the very virtuous do?' In Thackeray's work the 'virtuous' are often merely the 'self-righteous'.

The next essay, 'Small-Beer Chronicle', is devoted to another delicate distinction, this time to be made between ambition and pretension, between a virtuous desire to better oneself and a corrupt attempt to pass oneself off as better than one in fact is. But the difference thus stated is too stark and clear, for 'the beginning of this hypocrisy – a desire to excel… – is a virtuous and noble ambition' (216). That is how close base pretension is to noble ambition. At bottom, the question here is the same as that about class in 'On the Chalk Mark on the Door': what is the real nature of the person – of the wine, to use the essay's figure of claret which '*would be port if it could*!' Can claret – which is to say, the ordinary person – know itself well enough to make an accurate identification? Can other persons be accurate in their identification of quality? Surely most of us can see when claret is trying to pass itself off as port. Or can we? It is clear that the author of this essay thought he had made an accurate identification of the humbug revealed in the American artist Benjamin West's boast on a visit to France: 'I remarked how many people turned round to look at *me*. This shows the respect of the French for the fine arts.' But two sentences later he admits, ambiguously, that when he 'saw West's pictures at Philadelphia, I looked at them with astonishment and awe.' Was that because West had garnered such a great reputation on the basis of so little quality? Or was it that the pictures were so much greater than the humbug the author had thought the artist to be? Was he claret or port? Ambitious or a humbug? Who is to know? But, the essayist remarks, we are all eager enough to judge. We erect outlandish statues to heroes whose reputations are gone long before the statues fall, but, ask anyone about his competitor and hear him say: 'Ordinaire, my good fellow, ordinaire, with a port-wine label!' (229). 'Portifying' heroes and 'clareting' our competition are natural, routine acts most people undertake without recognizing the impossibility of knowing for sure. The moral of these sermons reverberate in the sound box created by Thackeray's doubts about self, about knowledge, and about certainty.

And so we come once again to the question, what led Thackeray to this unusual frame of mind? His contemporaries are not famous for the charity engendered by self-doubt. Carlyle, Dickens, Arnold, Tennyson are rather famous for having defeated self-doubt, for having conquered nameless fear, overcome humiliation, sounded the universal touchstones, and stood in defiance of cold reason to say, 'I have felt' in tones that silence opposition. Where is Thackeray's manifesto of faith?

Well, it is in these essays that say, 'are you sure?' It is in *The History of Pendennis* in the mouth of Arthur Pendennis when he recounts the tale of two brothers, each truth impelled, who choose, the one to enter the Roman Church, and the other to declare his atheism, for both are living, as are all mankind, in a world where knowledge is an uncertainty: self-knowledge, knowledge of one's neighbor, knowledge of the past, and, of course, knowledge of the future, knowledge of motives and even of the facts 'revealing' motives – all are alike subject to distortion, fatal incompleteness and falsity. It is a bold and foolhardy man, Thackeray seems constantly to say, who asserts the truth of his memory or of his facts or of his judgments.

Thackeray's manifesto of faith declares that less evil is done by kindly tolerance of peccadilloes than by righteous condemnation of half understood behavior. And yet there is clearly identifiable evil in the world. It is full of ogres and monsters, of wife murderers and husband killers, of child tormentors, and of vain humbugs and abject hypocrites. We are now confronted by two questions. What caused Thackeray to see the world as he did, and how could he, who saw the uncertainty of all knowledge, know so certainly that evil exists in these forms?

The answer to the first question lies, as I have repeatedly noticed, in the sorrows of his hopeful youth: the ordinary, though difficult, school experiences, the hope and loss of his patrimony, the wild escapades and health consequences of his college days, the passionate genuineness of his disastrous marriage, the loss of his wife, his 10-year long literary hacksmanship, the tantalizing frustration of his love for Mrs Brookfield and Sally Baxter, his friendship with Mrs Caroline Norton and his difficult but successful parenting of Anne and Minnie. These landmark experiences helped to shape Thackeray's view of his world – one he could not believe in implicitly, one he had learned to see through and yet to use, one in which he saw himself mirrored and which he constantly exposed.

Perhaps more important than this list of crises are the opposing influences represented on the one hand by his Evangelical upbringing and on the other by his youthful interest in the philosophy of Victor Cousin. His mother exerted enormous influence over the young man, insisting on his attendance to a series of spiritual advisers of the strictest order. Her own motherly instincts were generous and fond, but her ability to lay 'guilt trips' – in a more modern phrase – upon Thackeray were legendary. She was judgmental, narrow, righteous. She was like Helen Pendennis, whose notion of what her son should be and of what a paragon he was, could so easily turn to ready condemnation on the basis of unsubstantiated gossip – quick to love and quick to judge. His mother represented for Thackeray the largest and narrowest of hearts, an absolute certainty in the rightness of the narrowest interpretations of Holy Scripture. It is not unnatural that Thackeray chaffed against such teachings and behavior or that he understood in every detail the propensity of youth to escape parental restrictions. His first youthful rebellions are the ordinary ones of thoughtless, exuberant escape to freedom, to pleasure, to excesses.

But adversity has a way of focusing freedom and Thackeray was not one to crawl back into the parental cocoon for comfort. His ordinary British education had engendered an ordinary British pride in self-reliance, or pride mixed with shame, as we see in Pendennis, whose moral and pecuniary debts to the lowly Laura Bell drive him back to the university to obtain his degree in relative obscurity and to attack life in London on a reduced but purposeful level. Thackeray never finished his university degree, but he read Cousin, and Goethe and Schiller – in fact his education can never be said to have stopped, for he delighted in reading history and philosophy as well as fiction. But Cousin had a very important effect on Thackeray, balancing the influence of Evangelical Christianity.

Victor Cousin's *Cours de l'histoire de la philosophie* was published in 1829 from a series of lectures given in Paris that proved wildly popular with young French intellectuals. In 1832 Thackeray read the lectures in French, noting in his diary, 'Read Cousin's History of Philosophy.... The excitement of metaphysics must equal almost that of gambling at least I found myself giving utterance to a great number of fine speeches & imagining many wild theories wh. I found it impossible to express on paper.'[83] These are strong words from a man as attracted to gambling as Thackeray was. Cousin is not now considered a very important philosopher, but he popularized ideas that have had a lasting impact. Certainly Thackeray responded to several key ideas in Cousin's work that appealed to him, probably, in direct contrast to the dogmas of his strict evangelical Christian upbringing.

Most easily traced in Thackeray's work and in his personality is Cousin's basic idea of 'universal sympathy' or general tolerance. 'After having... proclaimed the supremacy of Philosophy, we hasten to add that it is essentially tolerant.... In fact philosophy is the understanding and explanation of all things. Of what, then, aside from error and crime, can it be the enemy?'.[84] For Cousin each person's limitations prevent the individual from a comprehensive knowledge of truth, which is parceled out, so to speak among the many. It is essential, then, to find the truth in the diversity of humanity; for Cousin claimed 'that every system contains a part of the truth; that there is no need to discover truth, only to unite its scattered fragments'.[85] One seeks the truth in others rather than seeking the false or that which is to be rejected. One becomes inclusive of rather than exclusive of others. This idea must have struck Thackeray with a force of recognition, for he was already indisposed to the judgmentalism and principle of exclusion which he found dominant in the Old Testament and that was preached by his mother's favorite spiritual leaders.

It follows from this first proposition that each individual's limitations and mental isolation must prevent absolutism and rigid dogmas. On the contrary, of those who claim to know the truth or feel passionately for a particular cause, one suspects that a narrowness of thought or ulterior motives drive the zealot. Thackeray had cautioned his daughter Anne, quoted in chapter 6, 'The Lord ordered Robespierre to set the guillotine up a Jehu Napoleon to slaughter the people before St Roch just in the same way – And you may read the Hebrew scriptures rationally or literally as you like.'[86] Just so Pendennis remarks to George Warrington: 'Make a faith or dogma absolute, and persecution becomes a logical consequence; and Dominic burns a Jew, or Calvin an Arian, or Nero a Christian, or Elizabeth or Mary a Papist or Protestant; or their father both or either, according to his humour; and acting without any pangs of remorse, – but on the contrary, with strict notions of duty fulfilled. Make dogma absolute, and to inflict or to suffer death becomes easy and necessary.'[87]

Cousin seems to have thought that eclecticism, or a pooling of all the individual truths would lead to a comprehensive truth, but Thackeray never espoused this idea. The limitations of each individual, the inability to understand or to know exactly what goes on in the head of wife or son or husband or friend will prevent us ever reaching a comprehensive truth – which, if we thought we could reach, would lead to the same evils of absolutism from which Thackeray fled. The thought is echoed time and again in his rejection of judgmental attitudes: 'and, as for your wife – O philosophic reader, answer and say, – Do you tell *her* all? Ah, sir – a distinct universe walks about under your hat and under mine – all things in nature are different to each – the woman we look at has not the same features, the dish we eat from has not the same taste to the one and the other – you and I are but a pair of infinite isolations with some fellow-islands a little more or less near to us.'[88]

The result of this isolation was for Thackeray that one could never judge another rightly. It did not keep him from forming opinions about others, but it did keep him from ever claiming he was right. No less did it keep him from having personal principles, beliefs, or a sense of integrity. But for Thackeray these were personal and private, not universal; whatever one's own personal convictions might be, one does not try to impose on others one's own limited view of the universe, truth, morality, politics or religion. As Cousin put it, 'Men are scarcely ever more than halves and quarters of men; who, unable to understand, accuse each other' and whose only means of arriving at tolerance or universal sympathy is to 'get rid of every exclusive prepossession' and to 'embrace all the elements of thought, and thus reconstruct the whole edifice of humanity in your own minds.'[89] Robert Colby recently remarked: 'Thackeray's moral relativism, an attitude that some have attributed to indifference or pococurantism on his part, is more properly interpreted as part of his eclectic outlook, his attempt to illuminate man's confusion out of the cumulated wisdom and folly of the ages ... '.[90]

# 9
# The Writer and Illustrator

The profession Thackeray chose to follow was not a very old one. Writing, of course, is an ancient craft, and authoring goes back as long as writing. But the profession – the life-sustaining bread-winning pursuit of writing and publishing – dates from as recently as Samuel Johnson in the 18th-century, before which men of letters were dependent on the good will of a patron. Writing was also a gentleman's pursuit, undertaken for pleasure or to impress one's circle of acquaintance. Accepting money for writing was tantamount to setting up as a tradesman. Lord Byron, who could have used the money, gave the proceeds of his writing away rather than have it thought that he wrote for money – and that was just 10 or 20 years before Thackeray's life in the profession began. But there was a growing sense, also, that writers, even those who wrote for a living, had pride and profession and independence as well. Johnson famously remarked to one would-be patron of his own that he was alike indifferent to his praise or his blame: an attitude and a declaration of independence that threw Johnson on the resources of his pen and his ability to please publishers and public.

Thackeray's aspirations to write and paint, when he was yet young and an heir, were of the gentlemanly sort, acceptable pastimes but unacceptable professions. And yet the climate was changing. Sir Walter Scott, who had initially thought the 'profits of my literary labour' were a convenience, not a necessity, soon found that the convenience was necessary. And yet many of England's best known writers of the 19th-century did not rely entirely on their writings for their income: Wordsworth, Shelley, Scott, Austen, the Brontës,

George Eliot, Tennyson, Browning, Arnold, Ruskin – all these had other sources of livelihood, though their incomes from writing were very important to them. Thackeray thought he had an inheritance to fall back upon, but it failed him. He tried briefly to develop the law as both a more respectable and more reliable source of income, but he failed the law – his heart was not in it – and so it failed him. Young Philip Firmin, in *The Adventures of Philip*, has about the same upbringing that Thackeray had had, with the rudiments of a law education. Philip actually gets some briefs and law business for which he is paid – an event that, as far as we know, never happened to Thackeray. But Philip too finds his life's work in writing rather than the law – and, of course, in the mock melodramatic ending of that novel, he also gets a legacy thanks to the discovery of an old will. Thackeray may have hoped for such a will, in the absence of an Aunt like Miss Crawley to leave him a more comfortable competence, but of course it never happened.

A man or woman without capital could set up in business as a writer, as Thackeray noted in *The Newcomes*:

> The drawbacks and penalties attendant upon our profession are taken into full account, as we well know, by literary men, and their friends. Our poverty, hardships, and disappointments are set forth with great emphasis, and often with too great truth by those who speak of us; but there are advantages belonging to our trade which are passed over, I think by some of those who exercise it, and for which, in striking the balance of our accounts, we are not always duly thankful. We have no patron, so to speak – we sit in ante-chambers no more, waiting the present of a few guineas from my lord; in return for a fulsome dedication. We sell our wares to the book purveyor, between whom and us there is no greater obligation than between him and his paper-maker or printer. In the great towns in our country, immense stores of books are provided for us, with librarians to class them, kind attendants to wait upon us, and comfortable appliances to study. We require scarce any capital wherewith to exercise our trade. What other so called learned profession is equally fortunate? A doctor, for example, after carefully and expensively educating himself, must invest in house furniture, horses, carriage, and men-servants, before the public patient will think of calling him in.

> I am told that such gentlemen have to coax and wheedle dowagers, to humour hypochondriacs, to practise a score of little subsidiary arts in order to make that of healing profitable. How many many hundreds of pounds has a barrister to sink upon his stock in trade before his returns are available? There are the costly charges of university education – the costly chambers in the Inn of court – certain expenses all to be defrayed before the possible client makes his appearance, and the chance of fame or competency arrives. The prizes are great, to be sure, in the law, but what a prodigious sum the lottery ticket costs! If a man of letters cannot win, neither does he risk so much. Let us speak of our trade as we find it, and not be too eager in calling out for public compassion.[91]

It has been estimated that 3500 different writers published at least one novel in the Victorian period. Although there is no listing of them, it has been variously estimated that between 40 000 and 50 000 novels were published from 1830 to 1900. It did not require a license, education, training or very much talent to write a novel, and one wonders how many were written and never published. But for those who could do it well and often, the profession of novel writing grew throughout the century.

*Figure 9.1* Vignette of Othello smothering Desdemona for ch. 25, titled 'Contains both Love and Jealousy', *Pendennis*, I, 235

Of Thackeray's likeable young male characters, George Warrington, Arthur Pendennis and Philip Firmin become journalists and think of themselves as literary men. Pendennis, of course, also becomes a novelist, writing not only the fictional novel *Leaves from the Life of Walter Lorraine* but also Thackeray's own later novels. Though it was easy to get into the novel-writing game, it took hard work to remain there. In *Pendennis*, a work many writers since then have credited with having inspired them to become writers themselves, Thackeray is pretty honest about the difficulties:

> A literary man has often to work for his bread against time, or against his will, or in spite of his health, or of his indolence, or of his repugnance to the subject on which he is called to exert himself, just like any other daily toiler. When you want to make money by Pegasus, (as he must, perhaps, who has no other saleable property) farewell poetry and aerial flights: Pegasus only rises now like Mr. Green's balloon, at periods advertised before-hand, and when the spectator's money has been paid. Pegasus trots in harness, over the stony pavement, and pulls a cart or a cab behind him. Often Pegasus does his work with panting sides and trembling knees, and not seldom gets a cut of the whip from his driver.
>
> Do not let us however, be too prodigal of our pity upon Pegasus. There is no reason why this animal should be exempt from labour, or illness, or decay, any more than any of the other creatures of God's world. If he gets the whip, Pegasus very often deserves it, and I for one am quite ready to protest with my friend, George Warrington, against the doctrine which some poetical sympathisers are inclined to put forward, viz., that men of letters, and what is called genius, are to be exempt from the prose duties of this daily, bread-wanting, tax-paying life, and are not to be made to work and pay like their neighbours.[92]

Mr Green's balloon was a hot air balloon that became a great and repeated spectacle at Vauxhall gardens. The spectacle of the newspaper or other periodical journals was, too, a great and repeated wonder. It had been less than 20 years, when Thackeray was a cub reporter, since the printing guild of London had staged a parade down the city streets in honor of the printing press, mounting some printing presses on carts and scattering freshly printed broadsides in

*Figure 9.2* Vignette for ch. 36, in which Pendennis becomes a published author, *Pendennis*, I, 347

praise of the press and journalism to the crowd as they passed. George Warrington pays tribute to the machines and the journals:

> There she is – the great engine – she never sleeps. She has her ambassadors in every quarter of the world – her couriers upon every road. Her officers march along with armies, and her envoys walk into statesmen's cabinets. They are ubiquitous. Yonder journal has an agent, at this minute, giving bribes at Madrid; and another inspecting the price of potatoes in Covent Garden. Look! here comes the Foreign Express galloping in. They will be able to give news to Downing Street tomorrow: funds will rise or fall, fortunes be made or lost; Lord B. will get up, and, holding the paper in his hand, and seeing the noble marquis in his place, will make a great speech; and – and Mr. Doolan will be called away from his supper at the Back Kitchen; for he is foreign sub-editor, and sees the mail on the newspaper sheet before he goes to his own.[93]

On more than one occasion, however, Thackeray's view of the 'great engine' was anything but flattering. To his mother, writing of his first modestly successful book, *Comic Tales*, he said, 'I hope that something good will come out of it all – something better than that odious magazine-work wh[ich] w[oul]d kill any writer in 6 years.'[94] And once, like George Warrington, walking by a printing house in New York, Thackeray is reported to have launched into a diatribe about printing presses chewing and eating the brains and life of writers. And yet one cannot escape the sense that Thackeray chose for his profession a work that he liked and could not have abandoned. In a speech at the annual meeting of the Royal Literary Fund in 1851 he admitted that:

> in my profession we get immense premiums.... Literary men are not by any means, at this present time, the most unfortunate and most degraded set of people whom they are sometimes represented to be... certain persons are constantly apt to bring forward or to believe in the existence, at this moment, of the miserable old literary hack of the time of George the Second, and bring him before us as the literary man of this day. I say that that disreputable old phantom ought to be hissed out of society. I don't believe in the literary man being obliged to resort to ignoble artifices and mean flatteries to get places at the tables of the great, and to enter into society upon sufferance.... As for pity being employed upon authors, especially in my branch of the profession, if you will but look at the novelists of the present day, I think you will see it is altogether out of the question to pity them.... Of course it is impossible for us to settle the mere prices by which the works of those who amuse the public are to be paid. I am perfectly aware that Signore Twankeydillo, of the Italian Opera, and Mademoiselle Petitpas of the Haymarket, will get a great deal more money in a week for the skilful exercise of their chest and toes than I, or you, or any gentleman here present, should be able to get by our brains and by weeks of hard labour.... We cannot help these differences in payment; we know there must be high and low payments in our trade, as in all trades; that there must be gluts of the market and over-production; and there must be successful machinery, and rivals, and brilliant importations from foreign countries; that there must be hands out of employ, and tribulation of workmen. But these ill-winds which afflict us blow fortunes to our successors. They are natural evils. It is the progress of the world, rather than any evil which we can remedy; and that is why I say this society acts most wisely and justly, in endeavouring to remedy, not the chronic distress, but the temporary evil; that it finds a man at the moment of the pinch of necessity, helps him a little, and gives

> him a 'God-speed,' and sends him on his way. For my own part, I have felt that necessity, and bent under that calamity; and it is because I have found friends who have nobly, with God's blessing, helped me at the moment of distress that I feel deeply interested in the ends of a Society which has for its object to help my brother in similar need.[95]

Philip Firmin will play out this paragraph perfectly 11 years later when his bad luck, pride, honesty and bullheadedness combine to lose him an inheritance, a job and a patronage. Nevertheless, he has friends and supporters who tide him through the low points until humility and good luck supply him again with work and a livelihood that will keep his wife and three children from the poor house. That literature brings its economic joys as well as its brushes with penury is celebrated by Pendennis as he speaks of the ups and downs in Philip's income from Mr Mugford and the *Pall Mall Gazette*:

> Had Philip possessed seven thousand pounds in the three per cents., his income would have been no greater than that which he drew from Mugford's faithful bank. Ah! how wonderful ways and means are! When I think how this very line, this very word, which I am writing represents money, I am lost in a respectful astonishment. A man takes his own case, as he says his own prayers, on behalf of himself and his family. I am paid, we will say, for the sake of illustration, at the rate of sixpence per line. With the words, 'Ah, how wonderful,' to the words 'per line' I can buy a loaf, a piece of butter, a jug of milk, a modicum of tea, – actually enough to make breakfast for the family; and the servants of the house; and the charwoman, *their* servant, can shake up the tea-leaves with a fresh supply of water, sop the crusts, and get a meal *tant bien que mal*. Wife, children, guests, servants, charwoman, we are all actually making a meal of Philip Firmin's bones as it were.

Well, Thackeray has been castigated for this paragraph, for killing time, padding his book and filling up space for the very crass purpose of making his money and neglecting the pure demands of the novelistic craft. But Philip and Pendennis are writers who benefit in the same way that Thackeray is celebrating here. Six pennies a line is, in fact, not far off the mark – witness an 1854 letter from Thackeray to the editor of *Punch* complaining of a low payment:

> A column of Punch contains 85 lines of 56 letters = 4760 letters.
> A page = 9520.
> A page of Newcomes contains 47 lines of 56 letters = 2612 letters.
> 4 pages = 10448.
> A page of Blackwood contains 60 lines of 56 letters = 3360.
> A page of Punch = say 3 pages of Blackwood. 4 of Newcomes.
> 3 pages of Blackwood at 5 guineas is 35 per page or £28 per sheet.[96]

Thirty-five shillings for a sixty-line page is seven pennies a line. That's how much Thackeray was dunning *Punch* for in 1854 and

*Figure 9.3* Instructions to the woodcarver for a drawing for *Lovel the Widower*: 'Make the oval regular & Time stepping out of the O', *Works, Centenary Biographical Edition*, ed. Anne Thackeray Ritchie (London: Smith, Elder, 1910–11), vol. 18, xlvi

when he didn't get it, he resigned. It was a profession he had mastered by that time. Unlike Philip, who did not know where to turn if the *Pall Mall Gazette* didn't need him, Thackeray had many outlets.

Besides writing for the magazines, Thackeray produced travel books of Ireland, Paris, the Middle East and London; he wrote Christmas books; he contributed to the Gift Books – (elaborately decorated volumes of illustrated poetry and stories for Christmas and special occasions); and he produced novels in one volume, two volumes, three volumes, and serialized as monthly parts. After 1848 reprints of his book appeared in 'cheap editions' and his magazine works appeared in three different collections of miscellanies in England, Germany and the United States. He remarked to one aspiring writer that before the publication of *Vanity Fair*, when he approached a publisher with the idea of reprinting some of his magazine pieces, he was turned away with a sneer, but afterward they were reprinted and made him £300 a year.

Though he was a failed painter and though he was turned down as the replacement illustrator for Charles Dickens's *Pickwick Papers*, Thackeray was a professional illustrator as well as writer. He contributed from 60 to 120 illustrations to articles other than his own, and he frequently illustrated his own contributions to *Punch Magazine*. More important, he illustrated three of his major novels. This is no small accomplishment, for *Vanity Fair* contains 186 illustrations besides the one on the serial wrappers; *Pendennis* has 210; and *The Virginians* has 144. He also illustrated his Christmas books, most famously *The Ring and Rose*, several of which were available in hand-colored form.

Many critics have faulted Thackeray as a draftsman, and no one has ever offered his illustrations as examples of the grace, beauty or technical skill that Victorian artists were able to achieve. But it is not difficult to prefer Thackeray's own drawing to those that the many artists, like C.E. Brock, George du Maurier, Edward Ardizzone or Harry Furniss, have provided as substitutes. Each of these artists can claim greater technical skill than Thackeray, but each seems to have been more interested in demonstrating his skill than in capturing the tone and essence of the fiction being illustrated. As can be seen from the illustrations scattered throughout this book, Thackeray's

*Figure 9.4* Self-portrait of the author gripping Time by the forelock. *Lovel the Widower* (London: Smith, Elder, 1861), 46

characters have no studied elegance. Their features and their costumes are not special. Pendennis may be the Prince of Fairoaks in the heart and mind of Helen and probably himself, but to the rest of us he looks quite ordinary. His behavior and the verbal description of his person suggest that Thackeray's artistic rendition of his appearance is not inaccurate. If the drawings undercut the heroic or fail to pull successfully at the heartstrings, one can argue that justice has been served.

Thackeray worked in two mediums with some variations in the processes: woodcuts and steel engraved plates. For woodcuts, he could draw directly on the block of wood – usually on a lightly chalked surface, remembering if possible to reverse the picture in case the left or right hand mattered; for the image on a printing surface produces a mirror image on the page. When he was done, an engraver at one of the many craftsman's shops in London would carve away the parts of the block that were not to print. Thackeray also from time to time simply drew the picture on a piece of paper

*Figure 9.5* Vignette for ch. 4, of Becky angling for Jos as a fat fish, *Vanity Fair*, 21

*Figure 9.6* Vignette of King Canute failing to turn back the tide, for ch. 5, in which Pendennis fails to stem the tide of love of Mrs Haller, *Pendennis*, I, 41

and relied upon the wood carvers to transfer the drawing to the wood. Either process depended for success upon the skill of the woodcarver. It is not entirely clear in every case of dismal craftsmanship if the fault lay with the artist or the woodcarver.

To prepare a steel engraved plate, the smoothed steel plate was covered with a thin layer of wax into which Thackeray would draw his picture with a stylus. The process was not simple, however; for having drawn those parts of the picture that would be the foreground and would require the darkest lines, the plate was dipped in an acid that ate away at the lines exposed by the stylus. A second operation with the stylus would expose more of the picture and a second dipping would eat away more lines in the plate. Each successive stage would reveal more and more background and each dipping would eat away metal, leaving the original lines deeper and wider than the last drawn lines. The effect was to give depth to the picture. As with the woodcuts, Thackeray would sometimes employ the services of craftsmen to transfer to the plate drawings he had executed on paper.[97]

The steel engraved plates were always printed on separate, heavier paper and tipped into the works as extra illustrations. The woodcuts were used in two ways, both of which took up space that would otherwise contain printed words. The steel plates and some of the woodcuts simply illustrated scenes from the novel. These woodcuts would interrupt the text and could take up as much as half a page or even more. In addition, every chapter began with an illustrated capital letter.[98] Very few of these vignette capitals illustrate scenes in the novel. Instead they are emblematic, many of them depicting scenes from biblical or classical literature that have a bearing on the story. King Canute fails to turn back the sea in several; the good Samaritan rescues the man fallen among thieves in several; scenes from the *Arabian Nights* show the old man of sea firmly gripping the sailor's back or a dreamer kicking over and breaking his wares in a demonstration of how people often bring about the failure of their own aspirations. Othello smothers Desdemona at the head of more than one chapter on jealously. And the egoistical letter 'I' frequently accompanies the representation of a person admiring himself in a mirror. Emblematic depictions of serpents, mermaids, sylphs, devils, and clowns seem to indicate that the events in the chapters to follow involve temptations, chicanery, or foolishness. And preceding the chapter in which Becky Sharp does her best to lure and land Jos

*Figure 9.7* Steel engraved plate of Becky's second appearance as Clytemnestra, *Vanity Fair*, 686

Sedley for a husband is an emblematic representation of a pretty maid fishing in a brook for a very fat fish. A Becky-like figure appears in the role of Napoleon gazing across the sea from St Helena Island before a chapter in which Becky longs to return to England denied to her by hers and Rawdon's debts.

Among the most famous illustrations to *Vanity Fair* is the steel engraved plate titled 'Becky's Second Appearance in the Character of Clytemnestra.' Jos Sedley, groveling under a painting of the Good

*Figure 9.8* Self-portrait as Napoleon in undated letter to Lady Russell, *Letters*, IV, 354

Samaritan, appeals to Dobbin for help while Becky hides behind a curtain with a diabolical look on her face and something ambiguous in her hand. Commentators on this illustration have said she holds a dagger or a vial of poison and most critics believe that the illustration proves what that text fails to say: that Becky murdered Jos, as the life insurance company suspects but is unable to prove.[99] Whether the illustration actually says what the text refuses to say is likely to be argued for ever. But it does seem to suggest that reading an unillustrated copy of *Vanity Fair* or any other author-illustrated book is the same as reading an abridged version.

# 10
# Personal and Literary Memorials

From the time Thackeray joined the Garrick Club in 1833, clubs featured prominently in his social life. That is where he maintained old friendships from college and formed new ones. His own wifeless home was not a convenient place of entertainment; so when he entertained, he often did so in his clubs or at restaurants. Even when he was working the hardest, he seldom wrote in the evening, when he often dined out in the home of friends or at a club. Talk was a necessary ingredient of Thackeray's 'research' for his writing, and he made acquaintances wherever he traveled. In the early days he joined societies – groups of young men who, not unlike the members of the debating club he joined at Cambridge, gathered periodically for talk. Among these tavern societies was the Eccentric, the Shakespeare and the Rationals. Later he found congenial fellowship in the Athenaeum Club, the Garrick Club and the Reform Club in London, and though only briefly in New York on the occasion of his lectures there, he spent many a Saturday evening as a guest of the Century Club, where his portrait still hangs.

Although he seldom joined any organization devoted to a cause, he did enlist in several causes as a young man, contributing cartoons and jibes to the Anti-Corn Law reform movement in the early 1840s, and he joined the Administrative Reform Society in the mid-1850s to support the movement to have civil service based on merit rather than patronage. This latter is an interesting turn of events since Thackeray had tried and failed to obtain the post of Assistant Secretary in the Post Office in September of 1848, just before the commencement of the serialization of *Pendennis*. And in 1857 he

*Figure 10.1* Vignette for ch. 64, of Becky as Napoleon gazing across the water from exile, *Vanity Fair*, 637

sought election to Parliament, without really claiming to merit a statesman's role. In his last years, when a great deal of daily mail came into the *Cornhill Magazine* and to Thackeray as its editor, there were many appeals to him to lend his name or his money or both to causes, which in those years he uniformly declined, though he was a soft touch for an individual in straights. But the social and professional clubs of London were both a solace and an inspiration for Thackeray, where conversation involved exchange of current ideas, political discussion and tale-telling and argument that sparked transmogrified accounts in his fiction and essays.

Of Thackeray's writing friends Francis Sylvester Mahony ('Father Prout'), Bryan Procter ('Barry Cornwall'), Jack Sheehan and Matthew James Higgins (Jacob Omnium) figure most pleasantly in his letters. He worked closely with illustrators George Cruickshank, John Leech (a friend since Charterhouse days), Richard Doyle and Fredrick Walker. He was initially very friendly with Charles Dickens, to whom in 1837 he had applied unsuccessfully for work as illustrator of *Pickwick Papers* when its original illustrator, George Buss, committed suicide. Thackeray clearly and genuinely enjoyed and praised Dickens's works in print, though privately he objected to the overblown writing style, and he remarked once that he thought

*Figure 10.2* Vignette of Napoleon gazing from Elba for 'Continental Snobs', *Punch*, 12 September 1846

Dickens was cool to him because he had 'found him out' as a poser. Though it was not always so, he got on fairly well with Dickens and his chief supporter and business associate, John Forster. Thackeray, unfortunately, brought the troubles on himself by caricaturing Forster in his letters to friends, a circumstance that of course became known to Forster, who of course objected. In 1847, club gossip led to a flare up over Forster's supposed remark that Thackeray was 'false as Hell,' but it was Forster not long afterward who brought Dr Elliotson to Thackeray's side when he fell deathly ill in October of 1849. A remark in *Pendennis*, three months after his recovery, however, opened the famous 'Dignity of Literature' controversy that revealed the deep rifts in thought, temperament, and, one would have said at the time, breeding that separated Thackeray from Dickens and Forster.

The 'Dignity of Literature' became a catch phrase for a number of festering discontents with Thackeray harbored by Charles Dickens and John Forster. They were the moving lights in what was called the 'Guild of Literature' in which they focused attempts to give professional writing a standing and respect in society such that the condition of 'indigent writer' would no longer exist. The idea was that the government would be asked to help support a pension system similar to one in France where grants or pensions would be available to writers or their families fallen upon hard times. Thackeray would not ally himself with the Guild of Literature in part because he was already involved in the Royal Literary Society whose approach to helping indigent writers was less ambitious – it offered small grants on a temporary basis to writers it considered capable of recovering a competence or to the widows and orphans of such worthy writers. Moreover, Thackeray believed the book purchasing public should be trusted to winnow the good writers from those who should perhaps seek other means of livelihood. Somehow, this position was taken by Dickens and Forster, who clearly felt betrayed or undermined by Thackeray, to be a self-serving attitude that appealed snobishly to high society. When a character in *Pendennis* remarks that literary men read as little and know as little as most people, Forster took umbrage in print in his own magazine, *The Examiner.* Thackeray responded in *The Morning Chronicle* and the battle was pitched. From the point of view of Dickens and Forster, Thackeray was a snob; from his point of view they were merely ill-bred. Indeed, for writers like Dickens and Forster, their entire claim to social status rested upon their literary efforts. For Thackeray on the other hand, there was a respectably monied and educated pedigree and social standing predating the writing success.

The comments by Forster, the response by Thackeray, and counters by Forster left tempers simmering for years. They erupted again in 1858 when young Edmund Yates, a Dickens protege, published an unflattering description of Thackeray questioning his honor and veracity, to which Thackeray objected in part on the grounds that the attack was on his private person not his professional work and in part on the grounds that the only contact he had had with Yates was in the Garrick Club, where, Thackeray argued, men should be able to speak their minds without fear of being reported in the press. Dickens and Forster stood by Yates, who was, nevertheless, for breaching club confidence deprived of his club membership at the Garrick. These flare-ups, and the controversy with Douglas Jerrold of *Punch* over an 1851 political cartoon, and Thackeray's 1855 remark about *Punch* magazine being nothing without the artist John Leech, have led many commentators to believe that Thackeray was thin-skinned, able to dish out invective but unable to take any. There might be some truth in that view, for although Thackeray several times publically regretted his early attacks on Edward Bulwer Lytton and apologized for them, he had tilted not only at the writing style but at the mannerisms and appearance of the man.

*Figure 10.3* Self-portrait in letter to the Knightons saying he was about to depart England, July 1863, *Letters*, IV, fac. 288

In his correspondence to friends about these episodes, Thackeray always distinguished between satire directed toward writing styles or toward the logic of arguments or toward the political implications of behavior, being careful not to confuse those kinds of legitimate public attacks with the personal attacks involved in poking fun at a person's appearance or disparaging a person's honor. The former category was open for attack because it was what the writer claimed as stock in trade; the latter, personal, category should not be trespassed because it was private territory. Perhaps there is some truth in the notion that Thackeray developed these principles after his youthful attacks on others and when he had grown big enough to attract similar unflattering attention to himself. In a brief lapse into self pity in a letter to his mother when *Vanity Fair* was in its seventh month and beginning to make a stir, he remarked:

> Jerrold hates me, Ainsworth hates me, Dickens mistrusts me, Forster says I am false as hell, and Bulwer curses me – he is the only one who has any reason – yes the others have a good one

> too as times go. I was the most popular man in the craft until within ab[ou]t 12 months – and behold I've begun to succeed.[100]

Be that as it may, because Thackeray's success led to renewals of school friendships with members of the aristocracy, such as Lord Houghton (Richard Milnes), and because he made many new friends among the social élite, the notion that he disparaged his profession to curry favor with the upper classes made quicker headway and has lasted longer than the idea deserves. In the 'Dignity of Literature' controversy part of Thackeray's argument denying that he curried favor with high society by disparaging his profession was that such a strategy would have been counterproductive, since it was his success in the writing profession that opened the doors to a society in which he felt at home – in ways Dickens never did.

Thackeray was a large man, 6 feet 3 inches, weighing about 230 pounds. His height kept him from looking rotund, but his round face, flattened nose, near-sighted squint and high forehead lent itself

*Figure 10.4* Self-portrait in letter to the Knightons reversing his direction to accept an invitation, July 1863, *Letters*, IV, fac. 289

to self-caricature. As a young man he affected a monocle and later signed many of his drawings with the figure of a pair of spectacles with crossed temples. By the age of 40, his hair was white, parted on the left and worn over his ears and collar. The fullest recorded description of his appearance occurs in Edmund Yates's unpleasant lampoon, but a number of photographs and drawings show him in typical unsmiling Victorian dignity, which belied the constant humor and comicality of his writings from beginning to end. His health was increasingly bad through the 1850s, plagued by the recurring stricture of the urethra that laid him up for days at a time. He worsened matters by overeating and drinking and avoiding exercise, though he enjoyed horseback riding and kept a horse. On 23 December 1863, after returning from dining out and before dressing for bed, he suffered a stroke and was found dead on his bed in the morning. His death at age 52 was entirely unexpected by his family, friends and the reading public. An estimated 7000 people attended his funeral at Kensington Gardens. Dickens, who had shaken his hand on the steps of the Reform Club a week earlier, wrote a generous memorial for *The Cornhill Magazine* of February 1864.

From the publication of *Vanity Fair* in 1847–48 to the First World War, Thackeray's reputation grew steadily. Never the bestseller that

*Figure 10.5* Self-portrait in letter to friend and critic Robert Bell, August 1860, *Letters*, IV, 198

Dickens was, he was more highly regarded than Dickens by readers who considered themselves more discriminating, such as Charlotte Brontë and Jane Welsh Carlyle and reviewers like Robert Bell and Lady Eastlake, but from the beginning there were detractors who preferred writers whose character portrayals were less ambiguous and whose grasp of and support for moral conventions were more comforting. Thackeray, like many good writers, was capable of exposing the hypocrisy and sham of conventional, socially acceptable behavior, but he had an unusual capacity, as well, to distrust his own and other people's best views. His ability to create detailed realistic images combined with an ability to detect sham or self-deceit in the best-intentioned acts led one reviewer to compare Thackeray to a fly settling on a good dinner. More philosophically sophisticated readers appreciate Thackeray's constitutional inability to dominate readers through an imposed moral imperative. Thackeray was a man of principles and honor whose sense of guilt about his self-indulgences was balanced by a sense of honesty in acknowledging his appetites and finding some comfort in the fact that they were not unusual. His own and his characters' moral dilemmas and self-directed humor have endeared and repelled readers, according to their tastes, from the beginning.

Gordon N. Ray's two-volume biography (1955, 1958) remains the standard; his edition of Thackeray letters and private papers (4 vols, 1946) has been supplemented by Edgar Harden (2 vols, 1996). Ray's study of the living prototypes for Thackeray's fiction, *The Buried Life*, adds significantly to our knowledge of Thackeray's circle of acquaintance. Peter Shillingsburg's *Pegasus in Harness* details the economics and logistics of Thackeray's professional affairs with publishers, and Edgar Harden's studies of the lectures and the serial fiction provide detailed descriptions of Thackeray's methods of composition. There is no comprehensive bibliography: the longest listing of periodical and book materials is Lewis Melville's in *Thackeray: A Biography*, vol. 2 (1910); it is corrected and augmented, in so far as contributions to periodicals, etc, are concerned, by Edgar Harden, *A Checklist of Contributions by William Makepeace Thackeray to Newspapers, Periodicals, Books, and Serial Part Issues, 1828–1864*. The most detailed description of Thackeray's separately published books is Henry S. Van Duzer, *A Thackeray Library* (1919), which is well illustrated but in need of replacement. Peter Shillingsburg's 'Census of Imprints to 1865' in *Pegasus in Harness* lists the multiple printings of Thackeray's books, most of which remain to be described properly.

# Notes

1 *The Uses of Adversity* (New York: McGraw-Hill, 1955) and *The Age of Wisdom* (New York: McGraw-Hill, 1958).
2 *The Letters and Private Papers of William Makepeace Thackeray*, 4 vols, edited by Gordon Ray (Cambridge: Harvard University Press, 1946) and 2 vols, edited by Edgar Harden (New York: Garland, 1996).
3 The best of these biographies are Ann Monsarrat, *An Uneasy Victorian: Thackeray the Man* (London: Cassell, 1980); Catherine Peters, *Thackeray's Universe: Shifting Worlds of Imagination and Reality* (London: Faber, 1987); and Ina Ferris, *William Makepeace Thackeray* (Boston: Twayne, 1983).
4 G.U. Ellis, *Thackeray* (London: Duckworth, 1933); Peter K. Garrett, 'Thackeray: Seeing Double', *The Victorian Multiplot Novel* (New Haven: Yale University Press, 1980); Jack P. Rawlins, *Thackeray's Novels: A Fiction That is True* (Berkeley: University of California Press, 1974).
5 J. Sutherland, 'Dickens, Reade, *Hard Cash* and Maniac Wives', in *Victorian Fiction: Writers, Publishers, Readers* (New York: St. Martin's Press, 1995), pp. 55–86.
6 See correctives by Juliet McMaster, 'Thackeray's Things: Time's Local Habitation', in *The Victorian Experience: The Novelists*, edited by Richard A. Levine (Athens: Ohio University Press, 1976), pp. 49–86; and Rowland McMaster, *Thackeray's Cultural Frame of Reference: Allusion in* The Newcomes (Montreal: McGill-Queen's University Press, 1991). And see the two volumes of *Annotations for the Selected Works of William Makepeace Thackeray: The Complete Novels, the Major Non-Fictional Prose, and Selected Shorter Pieces*, edited by Edgar F. Harden (New York: Garland, 1990).
7 John Carey, *Thackeray: Prodigal Genius* (London: Faber, 1997); J.Y.T. Grieg, *Thackeray: A Reconsideration* (London: Oxford University Press, 1950); and Charles Whibley, *William Makepeace Thackeray* (Edinburgh: W. Blackwood, 1903).
8 Anthony Trollope, *Thackeray* (London: Macmillan, 1879), p. 19.
9 W.M. Thackeray, *The History of Pendennis* (1849–50) edited by Peter L. Shillingsburg (New York: Garland, 1991), II, pp. 236. The pagination is the same in the first edition.
10 The spelling of 'humourist' should, for American readers, suggest its origin in the study of the four 'humours', the components of personality. The study of the humours is a study of human personality. Hence, a humourist is a psychologist.
11 31 December 1830, *Letters*, I, pp. 137–8.
12 *Letters*, I, pp. 138–9.
13 May 1861, *Letters*, IV, pp. 237–8.

14 That is to say, he attended an exclusive private school, but not so exclusive as Eton, Harrow or Rugby.
15 *Letters*, I, pp. 21.
16 Lady Ritchie, *Blackstick Papers* (London: Smith, Elder, 1908), pp. 127–8.
17 *Letters*, I, pp. cxiv; *Adversity*, p. 63.
18 Ray, *Adversity*, p. 66.
19 *Adversity*, p. 70.
20 W.M. Thackeray, *Vanity Fair* (1847–8), edited by Peter L. Shillingsburg (New York: Garland, 1989), p. 464. The pagination is the same in the first edition.
21 *Adversity*, p. 97.
22 *Vanity Fair*, p. 36.
23 *Adversity*, pp. 84–6.
24 *Letters*, II, p. 256.
25 *Letters*, I, pp. 23–4.
26 *Pendennis*, I, 16–17.
27 *Vanity Fair*, p. 465.
28 *Vanity Fair*, p. 618.
29 *Letters*, I, p. 81.
30 *Letters*, I, p. 74.
31 *Letters*, I, p. 81.
32 *Letters*, I, p. 76.
33 *Letters*, I, p. 138.
34 *Adversity*, p. 128.
35 *Adversity*, p. 126.
36 *Britannia*, 5 June 1841, p. 363.
37 The book is now in the Ransom Humanities Research Center, Austin, Texas.
38 The most extensive account and analysis of Thackeray's time in Weimar and the German aspects of his entire career are in S.S. Prawer's, *Breeches and Metaphysics: Thackeray's German Discourse* (Oxford: Legenda, 1997).
39 Robert Colby's, *Thackeray's Canvass of Humanity* (Columbus: Ohio State University Press, 1979), offers the best account of Thackeray's response to Cousin's work.
40 Diary, 17 June 1832 *Letters,* I, p. 209. The evidence, again, is Thackeray's venereal disease, and veiled notations in his diary, vowing reformation from gambling and fornication.
41 *Letters*, I, p. 190.
42 *Letters*, II, p. 36.
43 Diary, 27 July 1841, *Letters*, II, p. 30.
44 *Letters*, II, pp. 185–6.
45 An excellent place to start reading about the lectures is Edgar F. Harden's *Thackeray's 'English Humourists' and 'Four Georges'* (Newark: University of Delaware Press, 1985).
46 Eyre Crowe, *With Thackeray in America* (London: Cassell, 1893), p. 66.
47 *Letters*, III, p. 131.
48 *Letters*, III, p. 366.

49 Whitwell Elwin, *Some Eighteenth Century Men of Letters*, 2 vols. (1902; rpt. Port Washington: Kennicat Press, 1970), I, p. 156.
50 The two most important scholarly and critical treatments of *The Newcomes* are R.D. McMaster's introduction to the scholarly edition of the novel (Ann Arbor: University of Michigan Press, 1996), and his *Thackeray's Cultural Frame of Reference* (Montreal: McGill-Queen's University Press, 1991).
51 *Letters*, III, p. 304.
52 Wise men.
53 *The Adventures of Philip* (London: Smith, Elder, 1863), ch. 8, p. 231.
54 *Letters, Supplement*, I, p. 574.
55 A good place to start reading about Smith is in Jenifer Glynn, *Prince of Publishers: A Biography of George Smith* (London: Allison and Busby, 1986).
56 *Letters*, II, p. 240.
57 Joan Stevens, in one of the most detailed explorations available of the historical contexts of the London of *Vanity Fair*, remarks about Thackeray's comments on the styles of clothes in regency London, as opposed to those current in 1848: 'The subtlety of this is lost on the twentieth-century readers, for whom all the costumes are alike "historical"' ('*Vanity Fair* and the London Skyline', *Costerus*, ns II [1974], p. 36).
58 Gordon N. Ray, *The Buried Life* (Cambridge: Harvard University Press, 1950), p. 36.
59 See the Norton Critical Edition of *Vanity Fair* (New York: W.W. Norton, 1994).
60 W.M. Thackeray, *The Newcomes* (1854–5), edited by Peter L. Shillingsburg (Ann Arbor: University of Michigan Press, 1996), II, p. 251.
61 Rotten boroughs were political entities with depleted population that retained the right to representatives in Parliament based on populations from the pre-industrial period. They were abolished in the Reform Bill of 1832.
62 The Keating Five were accused of 'insider trading' on Wall Street in the 1980s. These things have a tendency to drop from view rather quickly in our own time as well.
63 The word 'flat' replaced the word 'simpleton' in the MS.
64 *Letters*, II, p. 309.
65 *Letters*, II, p. 385.
66 From Charlotte Brontë's *Jane Eyre*, George Eliot's *Middlemarch*, Emily Brontë's *Wuthering Heights* and Charles Dickens's *Bleak House*, respectively.
67 26 July 1846, *Letters*, II, p. 204.
68 2 August 1864, *Letters*, II, pp. 205–7.
69 *Letters*, III, pp. 85–6.
70 *Letters*, III, pp. 93–5.
71 *Letters*, III, p. 141.
72 This letter has not survived.
73 *Letters*, II, p. 407.

74 See Lucy Baxter, ed., *Thackeray's Letters to an American Family* (New York, 1904); Ann Fripp Hampton, ed., *A Divided Heart: Letters of Sally Baxter Hampton* (Spartenburg, S.C., 1980); and *Supplement to Letters passim.*
75 *Letters*, II, p. 407.
76 One cannot recommend too highly a reading of Micael Clarke's *Thackeray and Women* (DeKalb: Northern Illinois University Press, 1995) upon which much of the account here of the Norton–Thackeray relationship is based.
77 See for example *Corrupt Relations: Dickens, Thackeray, Trollope, Collins and the Victorian Sexual System* by Richard Barichman, Susan MacDonald and Myra Stark (New York: Columbia University Press, 1982); Eve Kosofsky Sedgwick's *Sex, Politics, and Science in the Nineteenth-Century Novel* (Baltimore: Johns Hopkins University Press, 1986); and the best work on the subject, Micael Clarke's *Thackeray and Women.*
78 *Letters*, III, pp. 297–8. Pisistratus Caxton narrates *My Novel* (1853) by Bulwer-Lytton; but Thackeray might just as well have gotten the device from his own novels narrated by Esmond or Lyndon. Unlike the latter, however, Pen does not concentrate on his own story but stands, somewhat like the author, outside a story he only occasionally enters.
79 *Pendennis*, I, p. 8.
80 Preface to Book One of *The Adventures of Joseph Andrews* (1742).
81 Preface to the second edition of *Jane Eyre* (1848).
82 *The Roundabout Papers* (London: Smith, Elder, 1863), pp. 179–80.
83 22 August 1832, *Letters*, I, p. 225.
84 Quotations from Victor Cousin are taken from Robert A. Colby's excellent and more detailed account of Thackeray's indebtedness to Cousin in *Thackeray's Canvass of Humanity: An Author and His Public* (Columbus: Ohio State University Press, 1979), p. 30.
85 As quoted in Colby, p. 30.
86 October 1852, *Letters*, III, pp. 93–5.
87 *Pendennis*, II, p. 234.
88 *Pendennis*, I, p. 143.
89 As quoted in Colby, p. 32.
90 Colby, p. 51.
91 *The Newcomes*, I, pp. 315–16.
92 *Pendennis*, I, pp. 353–4.
93 *Pendennis*, I, p. 308.
94 *Letters*, I, p. 459.
95 Lewis Melville, *Thackeray: A Biography* (London: John Lane, 1910), 2, pp. 71–5.
96 *Letters, Supplement*, I, p. 667.
97 Excellent accounts of the processes are given by John Harvey, *Victorian Novelists and Their Illustrators* (London: Sidgwick and Jackson, 1970); Nicholas Pickwoad in essays on Thackeray as illustrator in *Vanity Fair* (New York: Garland, 1989), pp. 641–7; *Pendennis* (New York: Garland, 1991), II, pp. 399–403; and *The Yellowplush Correspondence* (New York: Garland, 1991), pp. 151–61.

98 Every chapter, that is, except chapter 8 of *Vanity Fair*, which begins with a large centered illustration not including a capital letter, perhaps because the wood block broke and a substitution had to be made. Joan Stevens provides an excellent extended account of Thackeray's capital illustrations in 'Thackeray's Pictorial Capitals', *Costerus*, ns II (1974), pp. 113–40.

99 See particularly Teona Tone Gneiting, 'The Pencil's Role in Vanity Fair', *Huntington Library Quarterly*, 39 (1976), pp. 171–202.

100 *Letters*, II, p. 308.

# Index